THE WORST NIGHT EVER

DAVE BARRY

ILLUSTRATED BY JON CANNELL

Disney • HYPERION
LOS ANGELES   NEW YORK

Printed in the United States of America
Reinforced binding

First Edition, April 2016
10 9 8 7 6 5 4 3 2 1
FAC-020093-16046

Library of Congress Cataloging-in-Publication Control Number: 2015030364

ISBN 978-1-4847- 0850-7

Visit www.DisneyBooks.com

For Sophie, the Best Daughter Ever

I still sometimes wonder what was the weirdest part.

Riding down South Dixie Highway, wearing Dylan Schweitzer's horse head, on a Vespa driven by a Wookiee—that was definitely weird.

But not as weird as the night when Matt and I first saw the dragon and it came charging straight at us.

Or what happened in the woods, when those things got loose, so many of them . . .

So much weirdness. And it all happened so fast. . . .

Okay, maybe I should go back to the beginning.

CHAPTER 1

y name is Wyatt Palmer. I'm fourteen, almost fifteen. I live in Miami, which can be a strange place, although usually my life is pretty normal. I say "usually" because a while back, in middle school, I was involved in this insane class trip that ended up—you might have heard about this—with me breaking the collarbone of the president of the United States. It wasn't my fault (really) and everything turned out okay; in fact, I got treated like kind of a hero, even though, trust me, I'm not a hero. Anyway, for a while that was a very big deal. But after a few months it got to be a smaller deal, and eventually it wasn't really much of a deal at all.

Which was fine with me, because I'm not in middle school anymore. I'm a freshman at Coral Cove High School (Home of the Fighting Conches). And the first thing I figured out about high school was, if you're a freshman, especially a smallish male freshman, you don't want to draw a lot of attention to yourself or act like you think you're a big deal. It's better to be kind of invisible for a while. Don't get me wrong: most of the kids at Cove are nice. But like in every school, there are some kids that you don't want noticing you.

At Cove, there were two kids you *really* didn't want noticing you.

The Bevin brothers.

Those would be Nick and Troy. They're twins, and they're both big, although Nick is a little bigger. They're seniors, but they could pass for college students. Their dad is a super-rich businessman in Miami, and they live in a giant mansion. They drive a tricked-out black Jeep with huge tires and a Miami Heat logo. They're big stars on the football and basketball teams. Also, in the opinion of a lot of girls, they're really hot. The Bevins totally agree with this opinion. They're always kind of posing, like they're models in a Hollister ad, graciously giving the rest of us inferior beings an opportunity to admire them.

You probably already figured this out: I don't like the Bevin brothers. This wouldn't have been a problem if they hadn't known who I was. I could have been just another lowly freshman in a herd of lowly freshmen flowing past them in the halls as they stood around being admired.

Unfortunately, the Bevin brothers knew exactly who I was.

We became acquainted during my second month at Coral Cove High, the week before Halloween. I took the bus as usual and walked onto the school grounds with Matt Diaz, who's my best friend even though he's an idiot (you will soon see why I say this). Before school starts, almost everyone hangs around outside in the big courtyard that's surrounded by the buildings. You talk with your friends, try to finish the homework you didn't finish the night before, and try to wake up because it's *way* too early. Miami public high schools start classes at seven twenty a.m. This is insane if you know anything about the biology of human teenagers. Our natural wake-up time is maybe one thirty in the afternoon. If you put us in a classroom at seven twenty a.m. and expect us to actually remember anything a teacher says, you are a little insane, or a school administrator.

Before classes started I usually hung out with a bunch of other freshmen I knew from middle school. We met near the door to the Health Sciences building, which was where they have classes for kids who want to be doctors or nurses or paramedics. They have these creepy life-size dummies in there that students are supposed to use for practicing medical stuff like taking blood pressure.

Some entertaining things have gone on in the courtyard. There was this one legendary incident a few years ago involving the scariest person at Coral Cove: Arlene "The Stinger" Metzinger, who is the principal as well as the strictest person in the solar system. The Stinger is a short but fierce woman who grew up in New York City and prides herself on not having been born yesterday. Which she definitely was not. She's been the principal at Cove since like the Roman Empire. But for a person of her age she has amazing eyesight. She can spot violations of the school dress code from seven miles away. It's like a super power. She patrols the school grounds every morning, and every minute or so she'll point and yell, "HEY!" She'll be pointing at some kid way off in the distance who isn't wearing an approved Coral Cove shirt, or doesn't have an ID badge, or has shorts that are too short, or whatever.

"YOU!" The Stinger will yell. "COME HERE." The kid will be like, *Who me?* And The Stinger will yell, "YES, YOU." Then the kid will trudge over, and The Stinger will give him or her a detention. She gives out like twenty-five detentions before school even starts. You never know when she's going to strike next.

So anyway, according to the legend, one spring morning

a few years ago The Stinger was patrolling the courtyard, and she spotted this kid on the second-floor balcony next to the media center. The kid was leaning with his back against the railing and wearing a tie-dyed shirt, which is definitely a violation of the Coral Cove dress code.

"HEY!" yelled The Stinger.

The kid didn't move.

"HEY!" yelled The Stinger again. "ON THE BALCONY. TURN AROUND. I'M TALKING TO YOU."

The kid still didn't move.

The Stinger, looking even madder than usual, started walking toward the balcony. Many people were watching. It was pretty obvious the kid was going to get more than one detention. Probably several detentions, plus the electric chair.

Now The Stinger was under the balcony.

"YOU TURN AROUND RIGHT NOW," she yelled.

Still nothing from the kid. The Stinger was right under him, glaring so hard it was a miracle the kid didn't burst into flames. Everybody in the courtyard was totally quiet.

Then the kid jumped off the balcony.

A lot of people screamed. Not just girls.

The kid landed on the concrete about two feet in front of The Stinger, who jumped backward an amazing distance for a person her age.

Then she and a bunch of other people ran to the kid,

who was lying there absolutely still, like a dead person.

Except it wasn't a person. It was a dummy from Health Sciences.

And the T-shirt it was wearing said **APRIL FOOL**, because this happened to be April 1. Somebody had put the shirt and a wig on the dummy, propped it against the balcony railing, crouched out of sight, and flung it off when The Stinger got close.

It was a pretty good prank. A lot of people laughed.

The Stinger was not one of them. She tried *really* hard to find out who did it, but she had no luck. She did, however, give out about fourteen million detentions over the next week. So the lesson was: *If you mess with The Stinger, everyone pays.*

Anyway, getting back to this particular morning in October: I was walking across the courtyard with my idiot best friend, Matthew Diaz, looking for the group of kids we hung out with. I was especially looking for Suzana Delgado, who's this girl I really like even though she's kind of out of my league. She's pretty and smart and really good at sports and anything else she does. In middle school, she was involved in that insane class trip, and even though I got most of the credit for being a hero, the truth is that she was way braver than me. But we came out of it as pretty good friends; we even went to our middle-school prom together, which was basically—I know how pathetic this sounds—the social high point of my life.

We were still friends in high school, but not as much as I wanted to be. I saw her sometimes, and she was always nice, but since she was popular and hot she was usually surrounded by a bunch of other popular and hot kids. Also there were more and more upperclassmen noticing her, guys I can't really compete with, guys with cars.

But sometimes in the morning she hangs around with the old middle-school clot of kids, and this morning I spotted her as Matt and I walked across the courtyard. Right then Matt said something that is a perfect example of why he's an idiot.

"I brought Frank," he said.

"You *what*?" I said.

I should explain here that Frank is a ferret.

"He's in my backpack," said Matt.

"*Why?*" I said.

"He gets lonely when I leave him at home."

"But he's a *ferret*."

"That doesn't mean he doesn't have feelings."

"You can't bring a ferret to school!"

"Nobody's gonna see him. He has food in there."

"You're an idiot, you know that?"

Before Matt could answer, we reached the group. Suzana

waved at me and smiled, which made this an excellent day so far. I went straight over to her.

"Guess what Matt did," I said.

"Something idiotic?"

Suzana knows Matt well.

"Correct," I said. "He brought Frank to school."

"Frank?"

"His ferret."

I expected her to laugh at that, but instead she said, "Oooh, I *love* ferrets! Matt, let me see!"

"I dunno," said Matt, looking around.

"Nobody's gonna know," said Suzana. "C'mon, *please?*"

She did that girl thing with her eyes that girls do that makes you want to do whatever it is they want you to do, especially if they look like Suzana.

"Okay," said Matt. "But don't let him get loose."

"Don't worry," said Suzana. She's the kind of person who never thinks anybody should worry.

Matt took off his backpack and unzipped it. Suzana looked inside.

"Ohmigod he's so *cute*," she said. "Can I hold him?"

Matt said, "I don't think that's—"

But Suzana was already reaching into the backpack. She pulled Frank out and held him up.

"OHMIGOD!" she said. "He is SO cute!"

Frank didn't look all that cute to me. He looked kind of like a rat. But Suzana was in love.

By now more kids were gathering around to see what was going on, so our clot was getting bigger. I felt a hand on my shoulder, then it shoved me sideways. I was going to say something—probably a brilliant comeback like "Hey!"—but then I saw who the hand belonged to: Troy Bevin. He was with his brother, Nick. They wanted to see what was going on, and if you're standing between the Bevins and something they want to see, you're standing in the wrong place.

The Bevins shoved a couple more unimportant students aside so they could stand right next to Suzana, where she could be appropriately awed by their awesomeness. My excellent day was suddenly way less excellent.

Nick pointed at Frank. "Is that yours?" he asked Suzana.

"No, he's mine," said Matt.

Nick looked at Frank the way my mom looks at cockroaches right before she steps on them. Then he looked back at Suzana.

"I'm Nick," he said. He smiled at her, revealing several thousand perfect teeth.

Suzana blushed and said, "I know who you are." I wanted to puke.

Nick nodded like *Of COURSE you know who I am.* "What's your name?" he said.

"Suzana Delgado."

"You're a freshman?"

"Yes."

"Welcome to Coral Cove, Suzana Delgado." He made it sound like it was his personal high school.

"Thanks," said Suzana, blushing even redder.

"I'm Troy," said Troy. He also gifted her with a smile. So generous, the Bevin brothers.

"Hi," said Suzana.

"You like animals?" Troy said.

"Yes," said Suzana.

"You should come over to our house sometime. We have some amazing animals."

"Like what?"

"Exotic animals," said Nick.

"*Very* exotic," said Troy. "Way more interesting than a ferret. Mind if I take a look at him?"

He didn't wait for an answer. He just reached out and took Frank from Suzana. Matt started to say something, but decided not to. Matt's entire body is about the size of one of Troy's biceps.

Troy, holding Frank up, looked at Nick. "You know who'd love this?"

"I was thinking the same thing," said Nick. "Roxy."

"Who's Roxy?" said Suzana.

"More like *what's* Roxy," said Nick.

"Roxy would love this thing," said Troy, giving Frank a little squeeze. "For an appetizer."

"Can I please have my ferret back?" said Matt.

Troy didn't even glance at Matt. "So," he said to Suzana, "want to hang out sometime?"

Suzana blushed some more and smiled. I couldn't believe she couldn't see what jerks these guys were.

"Really," said Matt, "I'd like my ferret back." He touched Troy's arm. This was a mistake. Puny ninth-grade boys did *not* touch a Bevin brother.

Troy looked down at Matthew. "You want it back?"

"Yes, please," said Matt.

"Here you go," said Troy. He held Frank out. But when Matt reached for Frank, Troy suddenly tossed him toward Nick. The good news was, Nick, being athletic, caught Frank. The bad news was, Frank did not care for being tossed, so he bit Nick on the thumb.

Nick made a high-pitched noise, something you'd expect more from a third-grade girl than a Bevin brother. He jerked his arm, flinging Frank into the crowd.

"No!" said Matt. "Don't throw him!" He plunged into the crowd, dropping to his hands and knees, crawling through people's legs, looking for Frank. "Be careful!" he shouted. "Don't step on him!"

"Go ahead and step on it," said Nick, looking at his thumb, which was bleeding. "That thing *bit* me."

This is when things started to go really wrong.

The first thing that went wrong was I decided to say something. What I said, to Nick Bevin, was: "It bit you because your brother threw it."

That was a mistake. You don't criticize a Bevin brother, especially when he just let loose a girlish squeal and needs to get his macho back.

"What did you say?" Nick said, moving close and looming over me.

I don't know what I would have said next—probably something courageous like, "I'm sorry, please don't kill me, Mr. Bevin, sir"—but I didn't get to say anything, because just then everybody was frozen by the scariest sound a person can hear at Coral Cove High.

"HEY!"

The sound of The Stinger.

She was stalking toward us, somehow sensing with her supernatural Stinger powers that somebody was violating some Coral Cove rule. As she approached, there were shrieks from the crowd behind me, and people jumping aside. I turned around just in time to see Frank skitter out of the crowd through the forest of legs and scoot straight toward me. Without thinking, I bent over and scooped him up.

Which meant I was holding Frank when The Stinger reached us. Naturally her Stinger vision zeroed in on me.

"What is that?" she said.

"It's a ferret," I said.

She stared at me hard for a second, then said, "You're that boy, aren't you. The hero." The way she said it, it didn't sound like a compliment.

"I'm Wyatt Palmer," I said.

She nodded. "So tell me, Mr. Palmer. Why did you bring a ferret to school?"

"Um," I said. I admit this was not a brilliant answer, but the only other answer that came to mind—"It's not my ferret" —would have resulted in The Stinger asking me whose ferret it *was*, and I didn't want to rat out Matt, even though he's an idiot.

"Um?" said The Stinger. "That's your explanation?"

"Um, no," I said. Then, to make myself sound even stupider, which was not easy, I said, "I dunno."

She sighed, then looked at Nick Bevin holding his bleeding thumb. "Did that animal bite you?"

"Yes, ma'am," he said, looking sincere, hurt, and brave, all at the same time.

I said, "It bit him because they were throwing it around."

Big mistake. Both Bevins glared at me. Troy flexed his giant arm muscles in an unfriendly manner.

"Is that true?" The Stinger said to Nick. "Did you throw the ferret?"

Nick looked deeply hurt. "Absolutely not," he said. Which was technically true; he *caught* the ferret.

I said, "But he—"

"No more discussion, Mr. Palmer," said The Stinger. "You will get rid of that animal *right now.* . . ."

"But where can—"

"I don't *care* where. You will get it off school property immediately, and then you will report to my office."

She turned around and stalked away. Both Bevins were looming large over me now.

"You know what I like even less than ferrets?" said Troy.

"What?" said Nick.

"Rats," said Troy, staring at me.

At that moment Matt crawled out of the crowd. He looked up at me, saw Frank in my hands, and said, "You found him!"

"Yeah," I said. "I found him."

"Is he okay?" said Matt, standing up.

"He's fine," I said.

"Oh, good." Matt reached for Frank. But before I could

hand him over, Troy snatched him out of my hands.

"Hey," said Matt. "He's mine!"

"Yeah," said Troy. "But it bit my brother. We need to find out if it has any diseases or anything." He took off his backpack—it was an official Miami Heat backpack—unzipped it, and dropped Frank inside.

"You can't do that!" said Matt.

"I already did," said Troy, zipping the backpack closed.

"Give him back!" said Matt. He reached for Troy's backpack, but Troy shoved him with his forearm, casually, like Matt weighed nothing. Matt stumbled a few steps and almost fell. His face was red, and I could tell he was about to cry.

"Please," he said. "Give him back. He gets scared."

"Don't worry," said Nick. "It won't be scared for long." He looked at Troy, and they both smiled. These were not nice smiles. Matt looked at me like *What do I do?* I shook my head.

Troy turned to Suzana, who had been quiet during all the drama, which was not like her.

"So," Troy said, "we'll see you around, okay, Suzana?"

"Okay, sure," she said.

The Bevin brothers walked away. Matt started to follow them but stopped, because it was hopeless.

"What am I gonna do?" he said. "They took Frank!"

Ignoring him for the moment, I looked at Suzana. "You want to hang out with *those* guys?"

"Why not?" she said.

"Because they're jerks. Didn't you see them throw Frank?"

"They were just kidding around. Frank is fine."

"Seriously? Just kidding around?"

"But they *took* Frank!" said Matt.

"Because he bit Nick. I'm sure they'll give him back after they test him," she said.

"You *believe* them?" I said. "You seriously think they're gonna test him?"

"Yes, I do. And Matt shouldn't have brought him to school anyway."

I was staring at her. "So suddenly, you're big on rules."

She was staring back. "Wyatt, what's your *problem*?"

"My problem is, I think the reason you're defending those jerks is they're the famous popular Bevin brothers, and you really want them to like you even if they're jerks and they dump all over people who're supposed to be your friends."

"That's what you think?" she said. Her face was really red.

"Yeah. That's what I think."

"Fine. You think what you want."

She turned and walked away fast. The bell rang, which meant classes started in five minutes.

"What am I gonna do?" said Matt. "They took—"

"Matt, shut up, okay? I *know* they took Frank."

Matt gave me a hurt look. At this rate, by the end of the day I'd have no friends left.

"Look," I said. "I'm sorry. We'll figure out what to do about Frank."

"But what *can* we do?"

"I dunno," I said. "Right now I have to go see The Stinger."

Leaving Matt there looking sad, I trudged to the office to find out my fate.

CHAPTER

2

My fate turned out to be two detentions and a major lecture from The Stinger. The lecture was about how maybe I was a big hero in middle school, but if I thought that that was going to get me special treatment at Coral Cove High School, and especially if I thought I could violate the rules and bring a dangerous animal to school, I was very much mistaken, because that was NOT how Coral Cove High School operated. I tried to tell The Stinger that I didn't think I was a hero and didn't expect special treatment, but when I opened my mouth she said, "You are not here to speak, Mr. Palmer. You are here to *listen*."

So I listened until The Stinger was done lecturing me, then trudged to my first class, which was English with Ms. Padmore. This was my favorite class. For one thing, Ms. Padmore is from a Caribbean country called Trinidad and Tobago, so she has this accent that makes basically everything she says, including "Good morning," sound funny. When she reads Shakespeare, she's hilarious.

For another thing, this was my only class with Suzana.

Here's what I was hoping would happen. I was hoping that Suzana would have thought it over, and after the class she'd come up to me and tell me that she'd been wrong, and the Bevin brothers really were jerks, and she was sorry. Then we'd be friends again.

That's not what happened. When the class ended, Suzana didn't even look at me. She walked right past me on her way out and didn't say a word.

So that sucked.

After English, my next class—speaking of things that sucked—was Chemistry, which I hate. For one thing, the teacher, Mr. Krempler, is at least eight hundred years old, and he talks in this muffled voice, like he stuffed an entire tuna fish sandwich into his mouth that he hasn't gotten around to swallowing yet. So most of the time I can't understand him. And even when I can understand him, I can't really understand him, because he's talking about chemistry. I realize I'm only fourteen, but I'm already sure that whatever job I end up with when I grow up, I won't need to know the difference between a covalent bond and an ionic bond, or what the atomic number of Erbium is. I seriously doubt I'm ever going to have anything to do with Erbium, or Fermium, or Einsteinium, or any of the other "iums" that old Tuna Fish Mouth is always droning about.

After Chemistry I had Trigonometry, which is another subject I seriously doubt I'll ever need to know about later on. I was not doing well in Trigonometry. On the last test I got a D, which freaked out my mom, who checks my grades every day on the Internet. (Thanks a lot, Internet.) The day I got the D, my family was eating dinner in the kitchen and my mom said, "I see you got a D on your trigonometry test."

"Yeah," I said.

"You got a D?" said Taylor, who is my sister, unfortunately.

"On one test," I said.

"I never got a D in anything," said Taylor.

"Because you're in middle school," I said. "You're probably still learning the alphabet."

"No, I learned the alphabet already. It starts with the letter *A*. Which is the only grade I ever get."

Unfortunately this was true. It's one of the many annoying things about Taylor.

"That's right," said my mom. "Your sister gets excellent

grades. And I expect the same from you. Getting a D is unacceptable."

A lot of things are unacceptable to my mom.

"Well, I'm sorry," I said. "It was a hard test."

"Then you need to study harder," she said. "Instead of looking at your phone all the time." My mom blames my phone for everything.

"I *do* study," I said. "I just don't understand it."

"If you don't understand it, you should ask your father to help you. He's good at math."

My mom has been claiming for years, with no evidence, that my dad is good at math. The truth is that the last time he was helpful was when I was in second grade and trying to learn the multiplication tables. Dad was okay at those, except for nine times seven, which for some reason he always thought was fifty-eight.

But once I got to long division, my dad was basically use-less, because like everybody else he stopped doing long division by hand as soon as he stopped having to take tests on it. If he needs to divide something, he does it on his phone, like all the other grown-ups in the world. So he'd stare at one of my long-division problems for a while, looking totally lost, and finally I'd say, "Don't worry, I'll figure it out," and he'd say, "Good, because the only way you're going to learn is by doing it yourself," and then he'd go back to watching television.

But my mom still thinks he's this big math expert.

"Eddie," she said to my dad, "why don't you help Wyatt with his trigonometry?"

"What?" said my dad, who was watching *SportsCenter* on the TV next to the kitchen table.

"Wyatt got a D on his trigonometry test," said my mom.

"Yeah, he got a *D*," said Taylor, in case anybody forgot how annoying she is.

Dad attempted to give me a stern look without totally taking his eyes off the TV screen. "You need to study more," he said.

"I *do* study," I said. "I just don't get it. I don't even get what it's *for*. Like why do I need to know about the hypotenuse? When am I ever gonna use that?"

"It just so happens," said my dad, "that you use it all the time."

"I use the hypotenuse?"

"Every time you use a GPS. The GPS uses trigonometry to tell where you are." He looked pleased with himself, like it was actually him who invented the GPS.

"Wait a minute," I said. "You use a GPS, right?"

He nodded.

"So according to you, that means you use the hypotenuse, right?"

"Absolutely."

"Okay," I said. "So what *is* the hypotenuse?"

"Well," he said, "it's a . . . it's a mathematical . . . Okay, in a triangle, when you do a triangulation, you have your three, um, sides, and you, you *triangulate* them, and the hypotenuse is one of the, um, factors."

"In other words," I said, "you have no idea."

"Well not *now*," he said. "But I did when I took trigonometry." He went back to watching *SportsCenter*.

"So you think you're smarter than your teachers?" said my mom. "Is that what you think?"

"No! I just think they're teaching me stuff I don't need to know, just because *they* had to learn it." Which I think is basically the whole point of high school.

"Well you BETTER learn it," said my mom. "Because a D is unacceptable. Right, Eddie? Eddie? Tell him."

"Tell him what?" said my dad, who was watching a guy dunk over another guy.

"Tell him it's unacceptable."

"It's unacceptable," said my dad, not taking his eyes off the TV screen.

That's me: unacceptable.

Anyway, getting back to my horrible day at Coral Cove: After Trigonometry I had the one subject that I totally get the point of: lunch. I eat lunch with pretty much the same group of kids I hang out with in the morning before school, which sometimes includes Suzana. But she wasn't there, so I spent lunchtime listening to Matt saying how worried he was about his stupid ferret and asking me like eighteen thousand times how he could get him back.

The worst part of lunch was having to call my mom and tell her I needed a ride home from school because I had detention. She did not take it well.

"You got a DETENTION?" she said, loud enough that I had to hold my phone away from my ear.

"Actually," I said, "I got two detentions."

"YOU GOT TWO DETENTIONS?"

I would have heard that if my phone had been turned off.

"Yeah. So can you come pick me—"

"WHAT DID YOU DO?"

"Nothing. I was holding a ferret."

"YOU WERE HOLDING A *WHAT*?"

"A ferret."

"WHY DID YOU HAVE A FERRET AT SCHOOL?"

"It wasn't my—"

"THAT IS UNACCEPTABLE!!"

The conversation—if you can call it that—went on a while more, with my mom yelling so loud I'm surprised my phone didn't melt. In the end she said she would come and get me, but she would be late, and we were going to have a Serious Discussion on the way home.

So lunch wasn't so great.

The rest of the day also wasn't great, but at least nothing else really bad happened. After school I put my backpack in my locker and reported for detention at the office of the assistant principal, Mr. Forster, who is a very large, wide, squarish man, like a UPS truck that grew limbs and a head. There were fourteen of us serving detention. Mr. Forster took roll, then handed us each a pair of latex gloves and a garbage bag. He told us we'd be picking up trash for the next hour and he expected us to come up with our bags full, and if he saw anybody goofing off, that person would get two more detentions added on. Then he assigned us to different parts of the school grounds. I got the north side of the school buildings, behind the gym and next to the athletic field.

So I trudged out there with my garbage bag and started picking up trash, mostly discarded stuff from student lunches, including some seriously disgusting sandwiches that students decided not to eat, and I didn't blame them. After I'd been out there for about twenty minutes, the side door of the gym banged open and the football team came out, a herd of big guys wearing helmets and yelling at each other.

I wish I was good at sports. I played on a soccer team back when I was seven, but it didn't work out. Partly this was because my mom—surprise—was one of those moms that yelled a lot. This was embarrassing, especially since she didn't know anything about soccer, so the stuff she yelled wasn't helpful. Like she was always yelling, "Wyatt! Kick the ball! KICK THE BALL, WYATT!!" As if I didn't know I was

29

supposed to kick the ball. My mom yelled at me to kick the ball even when I was nowhere near the ball. Sometimes she yelled it when I wasn't even in the game.

The thing was, even when I did manage to kick the ball, I wasn't any good at it. The ball usually went in some direction that was a total surprise to me, as well as everybody else. So eventually I stopped playing soccer and tried baseball, but I was even worse at that, despite the expert guidance of my mom ("HIT THE BALL, WYATT!").

So I don't do organized sports. But I wish I did, especially now that I'm in high school. They have pep rallies for the sports teams where the band plays and the cheerleaders jump around and everybody cheers for the athletes, and I have to admit—this is embarrassing, but it's true—that it kind of makes me miss the way everybody cheered for me back in middle school when I was supposedly a hero.

I was definitely not a hero now. I was a loser freshman holding a bag full of disgusting sandwich remains while the football team ran past me. I kept my head down, trying to be invisible.

Which is why I didn't see Nick Bevin reach his hand out as he walked by, yank the bag out of my hands, and

30

heave it across the grass, sending garbage flying everywhere.

"Hey!" I said. I'm good with words.

"Oops," said Nick.

"Cleanup on aisle three," said Troy.

Hilarious, those Bevins.

They kept walking, and the rest of the team passed, leaving me standing there looking at a landscape of scattered sandwich parts. I grabbed the bag and started picking up garbage again, entertaining myself by imagining the Bevin brothers being dropped onto various sharp objects from various heights. I kept going until the bag was full and my hour was almost up and I smelled like the inside of a Dumpster on a hot day. Then I started back toward Mr. Forster's office. I was still thinking about how I was missing middle school. I was also thinking about what the Bevins would do to Matt's ferret, and whether there was any way to stop them.

That's what I was thinking about when I walked past the door to the gym, which was open. I stuck my head inside. The gym was empty. On the far right side was the entrance to the girls' locker room. On the left side was the entrance to the boys' locker room.

Which was where the football players changed into their practice uniforms.

Which meant they left their stuff in there.

Including their backpacks.

Including, maybe, Frank the ferret.

CHAPTER 3

I stepped away from the gym door and looked back toward the athletic field. The football team was out there sweating and lunging around and making grunting noises. It looked like they'd be there for a while. I checked the time on my phone; my mom wouldn't pick me up for another half hour.

I hurried back to Mr. Forster's office with my bag of garbage. He looked at the clock and said I could leave after I put the bag in the Dumpster in the parking lot. I put the bag in the Dumpster, then hurried back to the gym door. Out on the field, the football players were still grunting and lunging.

I looked into the gym. It was still empty. I crossed the

basketball court and went into the boys' locker room, which smelled like The Museum of Ancient BO. I didn't see anybody else in there. There were six big U-shaped groups of lockers with benches inside the U's. The first four were empty, but the fifth one had backpacks and other stuff piled all over the floor. I waded through it but didn't see a Miami Heat backpack.

I went around and stepped into the last group of lockers, which also had backpacks all over the floors. Right away I saw a Miami Heat logo on a backpack in front of a locker at the bottom of the U. I figured it had to be Troy Bevin's. I picked it up and was about to unzip it when I heard voices. I walked quickly back to the end of the lockers and poked my head around.

Football players, at the far end of the locker room, headed toward me. Practice was over.

I looked around for a way out, but there was no exit at this end of the locker room. Next to the last group of lockers was a door marked JANITOR. I scurried over to it and turned the knob. It was unlocked. I opened the door, stepped inside, closed the door. It was pitch-black, and it smelled like chemicals. I heard the voices getting closer.

Then I realized I was still holding Troy's backpack.

I opened the door a crack, thinking I could maybe toss the backpack out before anybody got close. But it was too late. Guys were already right outside. So I quietly closed the door and listened. My plan now was to wait for the players to get dressed and leave, then take Frank out of the backpack and get out of there. But for the moment all I could do was watch and listen.

I could hear pretty well through the closet door. Mostly I heard a lot of jokes I didn't get. As far as I could tell, the players were changing out of their uniforms, going to the showers, coming back and putting their regular clothes back on. After about twenty minutes they started leaving; I wasn't hearing so many voices. Finally I was hearing mainly two voices: the Bevin brothers. They were talking about Troy's backpack. Which I was still holding.

"I left it right here," one was saying. Troy, I figured.

"You sure?" That would be Nick.

"Yeah."

"You think somebody grabbed it by mistake?"

"Nah. It doesn't look like anybody else's. And nobody left theirs."

"So you think somebody stole it?"

"Yeah. And I think I know who."

"Who?"

"The little punk with the ferret. I bet he snuck in here while we were practicing."

"You think so?"

"Yeah."

"So why didn't he just take the ferret? Why'd he take the whole backpack?"

"I don't know. But I'm gonna kill him *and* his ferret."

They stopped talking then. I heard a locker door slam shut, hard. I was hardly breathing, holding totally still, waiting for the Bevins to leave, praying I wouldn't sneeze. They'd leave, I'd wait a few minutes, then I'd get out of there as fast as I could and meet my mom, who was going to pick me up any minute. She was probably waiting out there now. I just needed to hold tight until . . .

Oh no.

My phone was burping.

CHAPTER 4

"Did you hear that?" said Nick.

"Yeah," said Troy. "Sounded like somebody burping."

It was Homer Simpson. My ringtone was a recording of him burping. I yanked my phone out of my pocket to shut it off. I saw on the screen that it was my mom calling. She was probably in the school driveway, wondering where I was.

"It's coming from that closet," said Troy.

I looked around, which was stupid, because it was pitch-black inside the closet. From what I could remember, there was nowhere to hide in there anyway.

"Is somebody in there?" said Troy, his voice getting closer.

The doorknob turned. The door opened. There was Troy, wearing only a towel around his waist. Behind him was Nick, also wearing only a towel. Troy saw me, saw his backpack in my hand.

"You," he said, stepping toward me.

I didn't think about what I did next; I just did it. I threw the backpack at Troy. He did what people do when you throw something at him: he raised his hands to catch it. While he was doing that, I ran past him.

"Hold it!" he said. But I didn't hold it. Like I said, I'm not an athletic person. But over short distances I can move pretty fast, especially if I have a good reason, which I did now, because I could hear two sets of Bevin footsteps running behind me. They were gaining. Nick was yelling, "Stop!" and Troy was yelling, "I'm gonna kill you!" So together they were basically saying, "Stop so we can kill you," which is not really a logical argument for stopping. But I don't think the Bevins were into logic right then.

I hit the locker room door at full speed, opening it with a bang. That slowed me down a little. The Bevins were closer.

The gym was still empty. There were two main exit doors: the one I'd come in by, next to the practice field; and another one that opened onto the main school courtyard. The courtyard one was closer, so that's the one I aimed for, sprinting across the gym floor with two pairs of big bare feet pounding right behind me. Just as I reached the door, a hand—Troy's—grabbed my shoulder and yanked. I started to fall, but I had enough momentum to slam into the door, which banged open. I tumbled through the opening, landed on the sidewalk outside and rolled to a stop, curling into a ball in preparation for being killed by the Bevins.

Which is probably what would have happened, except that standing in the courtyard right outside the gym door were maybe twenty-five people, kids and grown-ups. It turned out that they were a tour group of eighth graders and their parents, checking out Coral Cove. The tour was led by two seniors. Everybody was staring at us: me curled up on the sidewalk; the Bevin brothers standing over me and suddenly realizing that they were wearing nothing except towels. They both turned red and scuttled quickly back through the gym doorway. A couple of kids were shooting video with their phones.

Troy looked down at me. Just before he slammed the gym door shut, he said, "You're dead."

"Are you okay?" one of the parents asked me.

"Yeah, I'm fine," I said, getting up and limping away as fast as I could. And I *was* fine, unless you counted the fact that my knee hurt and I was a dead person.

My phone was burping. My mom again, calling from in front of the school. She wanted to know why I didn't answer the phone before and why I'd kept her waiting for ten minutes and did I know she had to get home and make dinner and she was already late. I said I needed a couple more minutes to get my backpack from my locker.

In case you were wondering, that was unacceptable.

CHAPTER 5

It took maybe eleven seconds for a video of me and the Bevin brothers to show up on Instagram. I look pretty pathetic, lying on the ground, curled up and wincing in terror. But the Bevin brothers don't come off great, either. Their hair is wild from being in the shower, and their faces are red from being embarrassed, and when they run back through the gym door Nick's towel slips and there is definitely a visible flash of a hairy Bevin buttock. So all in all it's an uncool, non-Hollisterish look for them.

Naturally, because it featured the famous Bevin brothers, the video went majorly viral among Coral Cove students.

Probably ten people sent it to me, and everybody was watching it and laughing the next morning on the bus to school. The only person not talking about it was Matt, who was talking about Frank and how were we going to get him back.

I didn't see the Bevins in the school courtyard. I did see Suzana from a distance, and I was ready to smile at her if she looked at me, but she didn't look at me. She continued not looking at me in English class. Chemistry and Trig were the usual combination of boring and extremely mysterious. By the time lunch period came around I was starting to think there was a chance I would get through the day without getting killed. I was sitting at a picnic table with Matt and some other kids, eating a peanut-butter-and-banana sandwich, which I realize sounds weird but you should try it because it's really delicious. Suddenly everybody got quiet, like in a movie when the bad guys walk into a bar.

"Move," said a voice behind me. Troy's voice.

The other kids got up and moved away fast. Matt and I started to get up too, but we both felt hands on our shoulders pushing us back down.

"Sit," said Troy. Like we were dogs.

We sat. Troy and Nick went around the table and sat across from us. So now it was just the four of us, facing each other across the table, with many spectators spectating from a safe distance.

Troy leaned over the table toward me. His face was red, and I could see the muscles in his neck bulging in an angry manner. He put his face about an inch from mine. I still had a largish bite of sandwich in my mouth, but I wasn't sure what to do with it. This didn't seem like a time for chewing.

"You're dead," he said.

"You already told me," I mumbled. When I pronounced the *t* in "told" I spit out a little piece of banana, which landed on Troy's cheek, which made him even madder. He wiped it off and flicked it angrily at the spectator crowd, which parted to let it fly past—a little banana missile of rage.

"Yeah, but now I mean it," he said.

"The Instagram video," said Nick, jabbing his finger toward me. Even his finger had muscles. "You're gonna pay for that."

"But I didn't shoot that video!" I said, trying to swallow and talk at the same time. "I'm *in* it, remember?"

"Yeah," said Troy, "but the video exists because you tried to steal my backpack."

"I wasn't trying to steal your backpack!" I said. "I was trying to get his ferret back." I pointed at Matt, who decided this was his cue to speak. This is almost never a good thing, because as I may have mentioned, he's an idiot.

"If you don't give me back my ferret," Matt said, "I'm gonna call the police."

42

"Really?" said Troy. "You're gonna file a missing-ferret report with the police? I'll bet they'd drop everything and get right on that."

I had to admit, it did sound pretty stupid.

"Then I'll tell your parents," said Matt.

The Bevins actually laughed at that.

"You do that," said Nick. "You tell our parents."

Troy leaned toward Matt. "You really miss your little pet rat?"

"Yes," said Matt. I could see his eyes getting wet.

"We're taking good care of him," said Troy. He looked at Nick. "Show him."

Nick pulled out his phone, some kind of new one with a screen the size of a coffee table. He tapped it, then turned it around so Matt and I could see. It was a video of Frank, close up, being held in a hand. He looked nervous. Then the video zoomed out, and you saw why he looked nervous: he was being held over an open cage. Inside the cage was a snake.

A really, really large snake.

The hand moved; now it was holding Frank by the back of his neck, dangling him over the snake. Frank was wiggling and waving his legs around, like he wanted to run away, but of course he couldn't. The hand slowly lowered Frank toward the snake. The snake moved its head a little, like it was watching.

"That's a reticulated python," said Troy. "Beautiful animal."

"Her name is Roxy," said Nick. "She looks slow, right? You wouldn't believe how fast she moves when she's hungry."

"Which she is now," said Troy.

Matt looked away from the screen. "You didn't . . . Did you . . ." He couldn't finish.

"Nah," said Troy.

"Not yet," said Nick, turning the video off.

"But tonight," said Troy, "you'll want to be checking out Instagram."

"Roxy's *really* hungry," said Nick.

"No!" said Matt. "You can't!" He was crying now.

"Yes we can," said Troy.

"Okay," I said. "You win. You made a ninth grader cry. Good job. Now can he have his stupid ferret back?"

"He's not stupid!" said Matt, suddenly, idiotically, mad at *me*.

"I don't think so," said Troy.

"Why not?" I said. "You win! We're scared. We're pathetic. We're freshmen. You're the Bevin brothers."

"Exactly," said Troy. "We're the Bevin brothers, and you made us look bad."

"And that thing bit me," said Nick.

"Seriously?" I said. "A stupid"—I looked at Matt—"I mean, a harmless animal that is somebody's pet happens to bite you, because your brother *threw* it to you, and that means it's okay to feed it to a snake? Really?"

"Snakes gotta eat," said Troy.

I looked at Troy, then at Nick.

"Why are you sitting here?" I said. "If you're gonna beat me up, why don't you just do it? If you're gonna kill his ferret, why don't you just do it? Why did you come here and sit down to talk about it?" A thought bubbled up in my mind. "You know what I think?"

"No," said Troy. "What do you think?"

"I think you guys enjoy this. You *like* scaring us, just like you liked dangling the ferret over the snake. This is *fun* for you."

Troy looked at Nick. "What do you think, Nick? Is this fun for you?"

"It was," said Nick. "But now it's getting boring."

"Yeah," said Troy. "We're outta here." They got up.

"Please," said Matt. "Give him back, okay? Please. I'm really sorry he bit you."

"You'll be sorrier soon," said Nick.

And then the Bevins were walking away, leaving Matt staring at his lap so people wouldn't see he was crying. The Bevins moved through the crowd, which parted for them, everybody smiling at the two golden gods, everybody wanting their approval, nobody seeing the side of them Matt and

I just saw. While I was watching, Suzana strolled into view, looking sensational with two of her sensational-looking friends, the three of them and the two Bevins all gravitating naturally toward each other, forming a critical mass of attractive coolness, everybody laughing about something only they were cool enough to hear, Suzana putting her hand on Troy's large forearm muscles in reaction to something supposedly hilarious he said.

So lunch sucked.

I barely remember the rest of the day, because I was busy thinking about how crappy my life had suddenly become. After school I went to Mr. Forster's office and got my latex gloves and garbage bag so I could do my second detention. Mr. Forster told me to pick up garbage in the student parking lot. The good news was, this meant I wasn't near the football team. The bad news was, the garbage in the parking lot was even more disgusting from baking in the sun. It made yesterday's rotting-sandwich-parts-palooza smell like a French bakery.

So I was trudging around out there, picking up garbage and trying not to puke, when I saw Matt walking toward me with Victor Lopez. Victor went to middle school with us and was involved in the big class-trip mess. He's kind of serious, but he's a good guy, and he's really, really smart, especially about science and math. Like I bet he totally knows about the hypotenuse.

"Hey," I said.

"What's the smell?" said Victor.

"Me," I said.

"Whoa," said Victor, taking a step back.

"Okay," said Matt. "I have an idea."

This is almost never a good thing.

"What kind of idea?" I said.

"On how we get in," said Matt. He does this—acts like you know what he's talking about, when there's no reason why you would.

"Get in where?"

"Bay Estates."

Bay Estates is this super-fancy neighborhood with maybe ten houses in it. When I was in second grade I went to an Aladdin-themed birthday party there for this girl. They had an actual camel there, giving kids rides. The house was enormous. It had a game room *and* a movie theater. I got lost trying to find the bathroom. When my dad picked me up after the party, I asked him—remember, I was in second grade—if I could have a camel at my birthday party. He laughed and said probably not a whole camel, but if I was really, really good, he might be able to get hold of some camel poop. My dad thinks he's a riot.

But my point is, Bay Estates is where the absolute richest people in Miami live. It's surrounded by walls and canals, and it has a gated entrance with security guards.

"Why do you want to get into Bay Estates?" I asked Matt.

"Because that's where the Bevin brothers live."

"You want to go to their *house*?"

"Yes. I want to get Frank back. We need to go there tonight."

"Wait, *we*?"

"You don't want to help me?"

"Well, yes, I mean, I want to help, but going to their *house* . . ." I looked at Victor. "Are you in on this?"

"Sort of," he said, looking a little embarrassed. "I'm providing aerial reconnaissance."

"What?" I said.

"He has a drone," said Matt. "With a night-vision camera."

"I live across the canal from Bay Estates," said Victor. "I can control the drone from my backyard."

I stared at Victor—who, unlike Matt, is not an idiot. "So you think this is a good idea?"

"I didn't say that," he said.

"So you're doing it because . . ."

"Because I'll be in my backyard. You're the ones who'll be at the Bevin house."

"Wait a minute," I said. "Bay Estates has a security gate. We can't just walk in there. You have to tell the guard who you're visiting, and you have to be on a list, or they call the house to see if it's okay to let you in."

"We're not going in by the guard gate," said Matt.

"Then how are we going in?" I said.

So Matt explained his plan and asked me if I was in.

I thought for a second about the Bevin brothers, the way they looked at Matt when he begged them to let Frank go. Then I said I was in.

So I guess I'm the real idiot.

CHAPTER 6

"**W**atch out for alligators," said Matt.

"Right," I said.

"No, seriously," he said. "There's alligators in here."

"I know, but what am I supposed to do about it?"

"Don't fall in."

"Very helpful tip, thanks," I said. But I also shifted my feet a little bit so they were as far as possible from the edge of the paddleboard.

Paddleboards. That was Matt's plan. After dinner, I told my parents I was feeling kind of tired—planting the idea in their mind—then went to my room. After dark I checked back with them—they were binge-watching season four of *The Walking Dead*—and told them, over the sound of splattering zombie brains, that even though it was Friday night, I was going to bed.

Then I snuck out my bedroom window and rode my bike over to Matt's house.

He was waiting by the garage, inside which were two paddleboards. We rode with these, plus paddles, on our bikes, which wasn't easy, about half a mile to the canal that runs through Coral Gables past Bay Estates. We hid our bikes under a bridge, carried the paddleboards down the bank, and slid them into the canal. Then we got on them and started paddling toward Bay Estates.

This is when I started seriously wishing I'd told Matt I wasn't going to be part of the plan. The canal water was dark and creepy looking. The canal banks were steep on both sides, sometimes basically just walls of coral. We went past a bunch of houses. A lot of them had boats tied up to docks in the canal. The houses were up high above us on either side. They were all lit up, which only made it feel darker down in the canal. When we went under bridges there was no light at all.

And then Matt had to mention alligators. Which we actually do have in the canals. You don't see them that often, but they're there. I've even seen a shark. It was a small shark. But it was still a shark.

And the water was *really* black.

Finally we reached the bridge right before Bay Estates. We stopped under it and considered the situation up ahead. On the right side of the canal we could see the really bright lights that lit up the Bay Estates security gate. Past that on the right were the giant boats docked next to the giant mansions inside the development.

On the left side of the canal was a row of smaller boats docked next to smaller houses. This was the less-fancy neighborhood where Victor lived. Supposedly he was out in his backyard now. The plan was for Matt to call Victor's cell when we got to this bridge. Then the two of them would stay in touch by phone. Matt was wearing one of those Bluetooth

ear things that make everybody look ridiculous, but especially Matt.

He was calling Victor now.

"Hello?" he said. "It's me. We're at the bridge. . . . Right . . . Fourth house down. Got it. Okay." Matt looked at me. "You ready?"

"No," I said. I actually kind of meant it, but Matt took it as a joke and started paddling. I followed him, the two of us keeping to the right side of the canal, so anybody up on the bank wouldn't see us. We passed the guardhouse, and soon we were alongside the first Bay Estates house, which had a boat docked next to it that looked like a cruise ship. We kept going, Matt every now and then saying something to Victor. When we were between boats we saw huge lawns leading up to the hotel-size mansions of Bay Estates, with resort-size pools and patios with those serious outdoor kitchens that rich people never seem to actually cook anything in, but they have them anyway because they're expensive and all the other rich people have them.

When we got next to the third house Matt stopped paddling. I stopped behind him.

"Okay," he said into his Bluetooth thing.

"Victor's launching his drone," he told me.

We listened, drifting on our paddleboards. For a minute all I heard was water lapping against the boats. Then I heard a hum, and there it was, swooping over us, a four-blade drone, flying past the little sliver of moon.

"Victor sees us," said Matt. "Let's go."

We started paddling again, following the drone to the fourth house. This one had several boats out front—a huge one and a couple of smaller ones, which were still pretty big.

It also had something none of the other houses had: a wall. A *high* wall, ten feet at least. It ran next to the dock. In the middle there was a big, serious-looking steel door, closed.

"There's a wall," I said. This probably was not necessary.

"I know," said Matt.

"So if that door is locked, which I'm guessing it is, how are we supposed to get in?"

"Victor thinks we can get in by that tree." Matt pointed to the far end of the wall, where it turned a corner at the end of the dock. Just around the corner was a huge banyan tree, the kind that spreads out wide and has lots of big roots running down to the ground from branches. It was growing on the canal bank just inside the wall, but some of the roots had come down outside, like the tree was trying to swallow the wall. It did look like the tree might be climbable, which I have to admit made my heart sink a little, because I was starting to hope that we'd have to abandon our mission.

We paddled between two of the boats and moved along

the dock until we came to a ladder. We tossed our paddles onto the dock then climbed the ladder, dragging the paddleboards with us. We stood on the dock, looking around. I could just hear Victor's drone, hovering on the other side of the wall.

"Okay," whispered Matt into his Bluetooth thing.

"Victor says everything looks good," Matt whispered to me.

Easy for Victor to say, standing in his own backyard.

Just in case, I tried the knob on the big metal door. Locked. We dragged our paddleboards over to the banyan tree and leaned them against the wall, then looked at the tree roots. Victor was right: They were climbable. Matt didn't wait. He grabbed one and started up. He's a little guy and a fast climber. In ten seconds he was on top of the wall.

"You coming?" he whispered.

"Yeah," I said.

It took me a little longer to get to the top. I crouched next to Matt, the two of us looking out onto the Bevin compound. In the distance we could see the house, another gigantic mansion, like other ones in Bay Estates. What was different was the yard. The others were mostly lawns and landscaping, with lots of lighting.

The Bevin yard was dark.

We could make out some round shapes in the darkness—

big grass mounds, they looked like. But except for a few low, dim footpath lights, it was black out there.

"Why's it so dark?" I whispered.

"I dunno," said Matt. "Let's go find Frank."

He started climbing down, which was easier than coming up the other side, because we had the whole rest of the tree to use as a ladder. I followed him down into the darkness. A couple of things were on my mind. How exactly were we going to find Frank? We didn't have what I would call a detailed plan. We'd spent more time thinking about getting into the Bevin compound than what we'd do when we got there. We were hoping that once we got inside, we'd see a cage or something. But here in the darkness, inside the wall, we couldn't really see anything.

And that was the other thing: Why was it so dark?

And what was the reason for this huge wall? To keep people out?

Or to keep something in?

Matt started forward on what I guess was a path. I was right behind him. When he stopped, I almost bumped into him.

"What is it?" I whispered.

"It's Victor," he whispered. "He says somebody's coming."

CHAPTER 7

"Who's coming?" I whispered.

"Guys with flashlights," said Matt.

"Where are they?"

He held up a hand, telling me to be quiet while he listened on the Bluetooth.

"They're coming from the house," he whispered. "There's a path down the middle of the yard."

That was to our right.

"This way," I whispered, moving to the wall on the left side of the yard. There was a grass-covered mound there, maybe six feet high, a few yards from the wall. We went behind it and stopped. After a few seconds we could hear men's voices coming toward us.

"It's three guys," whispered Matt. "They're heading toward the dock."

We listened as the men went past, talking just loud enough so we could hear voices, but not loud enough so we could understand what they were saying. It didn't sound like the brothers, though. It sounded like older guys.

We heard the dock gate open, then close with a *CLUNK*.

"They're outside," said Matt.

"What are they doing? Are they getting on a boat?"

"No. They're just standing there on the dock. Let's go."

"Wait . . . Go where?"

"To find Frank."

"What about those guys?"

"They went that way. We're going this way." Matt started walking toward the house.

Ordinarily, Matt is the most chicken person I know who is not literally a chicken. But all of a sudden he was acting like some kind of ninja. Never underestimate a boy's love for his ferret, I guess. I wasn't thrilled about going toward the house with guys walking around outside, but I was less thrilled about being left alone in the dark. So I followed Matt.

We passed behind some more grass-covered mounds, stopping in the shadows at the edge of the last one. Ahead of us was the pool and patio area in back of the house. The house had a lot of big windows, and it was all lit up, so we could see most of the inside. The middle of the ground floor was a huge living room with wide marble stairs on the far side. To the right of that was what looked like a dining room. To the left was another big room that had a TV screen the size of a garage door. That room was dark, but the TV was on, showing *Fast and Furious 7*, the movie where a bunch of guys supposedly drive cars out of a cargo plane flying at ten thousand feet, which is actually one of the more realistic parts of the plot. The volume was cranked way up; it was loud even outside. We could see the back of a long sofa facing the screen, but we couldn't tell if anybody was on it.

We didn't see anybody in any of the upstairs windows.

"The bedrooms are probably upstairs," said Matt.

"You think that's where they'd have Frank?"

"I guess so."

Matt whispered into his Bluetooth, "Victor, are they still on the dock?"

Victor must've said yes, because Matt said to me, "Okay, let's go."

We left the shadows, walked around the pool, and hurried across the patio. We were totally visible if anybody was looking our way. I looked back toward the yard. I could see the footpath, lit by dim little lights near the ground running down to the dock. But I didn't see anybody on the footpath.

We were outside the living room. It had a set of big double doors. Matt tried one of the door handles. It turned; the door wasn't locked. He pulled the door open slowly. We were blasted by the soundtrack from *Fast and Furious*. Matt stepped into the living room. I followed. Just like that, we were *inside the Bevin brothers' house.*

You know how some people say that when they were in a really scary situation, they suddenly felt calm? That definitely did not happen to me. The only thing I suddenly felt was a strong urge to pee my pants. If I'd been alone I would have turned around and gotten the heck out of there.

But not Ninja Matt. He leaned close so I could hear him over the sound of *Fast and Furious 7*, looked me straight in the eye, and said, quote, "Let's do this."

Seriously, he said that. Like we were in a movie. Maybe he was inspired by *Fast and Furious 7*.

Then he turned and walked quickly across the living room to the stairs, with me jogging behind.

At the top of the stairs was a long hallway going in both directions, with doorways on both sides. The first door to our right was wide open. We looked inside: it was a bedroom—a big bedroom, with nobody in it. There were clothes scattered around the floor—Nick's or Troy's, it looked like. There was a big flat-screen TV mounted on the wall over a desk with a computer on it, next to an Apple watch—a gold one, with a black band—plugged into a charging cable. There was no sign of Frank.

There was another doorway directly across the hall. The door was closed. Matt and I looked at each other, then he kind of shrugged, turned the doorknob and opened the door. The room was dark, but by the light from the hall we could see that it was another bedroom, and there didn't seem to be anybody in it. It also had the flat-screen TV, the desk, the computer, the Apple watch, even the clothes on the floor. Messy fellows, those Bevin brothers.

Matt reached in and turned on the overhead light. We stepped in and looked around.

We both saw it at the same time, by the wall next to the desk.

The snake cage.

It was the one Nick showed Matt in the video on his phone, except now the top was closed. We walked over to it. Roxy the python was inside, coiled up, not moving. She looked even bigger in real life than she did in the video.

Then Matt made a little high-pitched sound, and I saw why. On the floor on the other side of Roxy's cage was another cage, a little wire one. Inside that cage—as opposed to inside Roxy—was Frank.

Matt opened the wire-cage door and took Frank out. I

guess Frank was happy to see Matt—it's hard to tell with a ferret—but Matt was definitely thrilled to see Frank. He actually kissed him. I know, ew, right? But that's how happy Matt was. Even I was feeling pretty good.

This feeling lasted maybe 2.7 seconds. Which is how long it took me to notice something.

"Listen," I whispered.

"What?" said Matt.

"Downstairs. Listen."

He cocked his head, listening with his non-Bluetooth ear. "I don't hear anything."

"Exactly. The movie must be over."

"Uh-oh," whispered Matt.

"Yeah," I whispered. "We better get—"

"*Shh,*" hissed Matt. He nodded his head toward the open bedroom door.

I listened, and there it was.

Footsteps, coming up the stairs.

And voices.

Bevin voices.

CHAPTER

8

att gave me a terrified look, like *What do we do?*
Apparently now that he had his ferret back he was no longer
Ninja Matt.

I looked toward the door we entered, which was a way
out, but which also led to the hallway, which is where the
Bevins would be in a few seconds. The voices were getting
closer.

We looked around. There were two other doors in the
bedroom, both closed. A closet and a bathroom, probably.

Footsteps in the hall, getting closer.

I grabbed Matt's arm and pulled him to the closest door. I

opened it: it was a big closet. I pulled Matt inside and closed the door as quietly as I could. It was totally black in there. I could feel Matt standing next to me, but I couldn't see him.

I heard somebody come into the bedroom. Then I heard the TV turn on, tuned to *SportsCenter*, which was all that I could hear for a little while. I realized that I wasn't breathing, so I decided it would be a good idea to start breathing again, as quietly as possible.

From next to me in the darkness I heard a tiny voice in Matt's Bluetooth earpiece. Matt leaned close to my ear and whispered, "Victor says a boat pulled up to the dock."

"Okay," I whispered.

"What are we gonna do?" he whispered.

"Hope he goes to sleep so we can sneak out of here." *Also pray he doesn't open the closet door*, I thought.

We listened to *SportsCenter* some more through the door. Then the TV went off.

"Hey, Troy!"

Matt and I both jumped. Nick's voice was so close it sounded like he was in the closet with us. Matt grabbed my arm.

"What?" answered Troy's muffled voice from across the hall.

"Did you open the ferret cage?"

"No. Why?"

"It's gone."

"What's gone?"

"The ferret."

"It's gone?" Troy's voice was closer. He was in the bed-room now.

"Yeah, and the cage door's open."

"You must've left it open."

"No, I didn't."

"What, you think it let itself out?"

"I don't know. I just know I didn't let it out."

"Maybe Roxy got it."

"No, her cage is closed. But when I find it I'm definitely gonna feed it to her. I should've done it when we got home."

Next to me in the dark I felt Matt tense up.

"Help me look for it," said Troy. "It has to be around here somewhere."

There were sounds of them moving around, opening and closing drawers. I was staring in the direction of the closet door, thinking sooner or later one of them would open it. I tugged on Matt's arm, pulling him toward the back of the closet. Feeling around for something to hide behind. I grabbed what felt like a shirt and pulled it in front of Matt and me. We had our backs pressed against the wall.

Then the closet door opened, and Nick was standing there. He was wearing shorts and no shirt. He looked like the Incredible Hulk, only more muscular.

I saw that what I'd grabbed was a T-shirt, and it didn't really cover me or Matt. Nick was going to see us the second he turned on the closet light. Which he was reaching his hand out to do.

We were dead.

Then Nick's phone rang.

His hand stopped an inch from the light switch. He pulled a phone from his shorts and said, "Yeah?" Then, "Okay."

"They're back," he said to Troy.

"Let's go," said Troy. "I want to see it."

Nick closed the closet door.

So we weren't dead.

Yet.

CHAPTER 9

e stayed in the closet another minute, making sure the Bevins were gone. I heard Matt's Bluetooth earpiece talking again.

"Victor says a boat came and dropped off some kind of big box at the dock. The three guys are wheeling it up the path."

"Ask him if he sees Troy and Nick," I whispered.

Matt whispered, "Do you see the Bevin brothers?" Victor said something in his ear.

"He says yeah," whispered Matt. "They just came out."

"Let's go," I said.

Matt put Frank in the front pouch of his hoodie. Then we hurried out of the bedroom and down the stairs. We stopped at the bottom to look around the living room. It was empty.

"Ask Victor where they are now," I said.

"Where are they now?" Matt said into his earpiece. After a pause, he told me, "They're on the path. Victor said they're all looking at the box, so we can leave now if we hurry."

We hurried across the living room and out the patio door. Straight ahead was the path down to the dock. It was dark, but I could see the shapes of people about two-thirds of the way down.

We ducked down and ran right, to the wall alongside the property that we followed coming up. It was dark next to the wall, which made me feel safer. All we had to do now was get back down to the dock.

"Tell Victor we're going to the dock, and to let us know if they move," I whispered.

Matt told Victor, and we started walking along the wall. The grass mounds kept us hidden from the path. Matt kept whispering into the Bluetooth, letting Matt know as we passed each mound. We heard men's voices coming from our left. We were getting closer to them. When we were passing behind the fourth mound, Matt put his hand on my arm and whispered, "Hold it."

"What?"

"Victor says be careful after we pass this hill because they might be able to see us from where they're standing. Also, he has to land the drone and change the batteries."

We crept forward until we were at the corner of the building. The voices were nearby and loud, guys telling each other to be careful about something.

I peeked my head out over the mound, just enough to see what was going on.

They were on the pathway, maybe twenty-five feet away: the Bevin brothers and three men I didn't recognize. They had flashlights and were gathered around a big crate, next to a mound on the other side of the path. When a flashlight beam flicked past it, I noticed something weird: the mound had a door. The outside of the door was covered with grass, so when it was closed it would blend into the rest of the mound. But now it was partly open, and I caught a glimpse of a tunnel going down under the mound. *What was down there? Why was the entrance hidden?*

Another question was, *What was inside the crate?* Whatever it was, the men were trying to get it out, and they were having trouble. One of them had a stick with a noose at the end, which he kept poking into the crate.

"What's happening?" whispered Matt, peeking over the mound.

"I don't know," I whispered. "There's some kind of—"

I was interrupted by shouting. The guy with the noose had got hold of whatever was inside the crate. He and another guy were pulling backward on it. These were big guys, but whatever was in there was giving them a battle.

They gave the pole a yank.

"Be careful!" Troy said. "Don't hurt it."

"We're trying not to," said one of the guys. "But this thing is *strong*."

They gave the pole another yank.

This time it worked. The men staggered backward, and out of the crate came a head.

"Whoa," said Matt, too surprised to whisper. "What *is* that?"

What it looked like was a dinosaur. It had a lizardish head, but way bigger than any lizard I ever saw—more like the size of an alligator. It was sticking out a tongue that had to be over a foot long. It did not like having the noose around its neck. It was shaking its head back and forth, trying to get loose, but the men were holding on.

Everybody was yelling now. The guys with the pole gave another yank and dragged more of the thing out. It was huge. It had weird wrinkly skin, and its front feet had *major* claws. Also it was extremely unhappy. Suddenly it opened its mouth and lunged forward. The two pole guys staggered back. The thing was heavy, and *strong*.

"Don't let it bite you!" shouted the third man, backing

away from the head, which was still whipping around, with the mouth open wide.

The pole guys got their balance again and gave another pull. This time the thing came all the way out of the crate.

"Ohmigod," said Matt.

It had to be ten feet long. Its rear feet had the same huge claws as the front ones. Its tail was massive. Its whole body was thrashing around now; the two guys holding the pole were struggling to control it. I was glad I wasn't standing next to it.

Now the pole guys were trying to maneuver the thing toward the doorway in the mound. This made the thing even more unhappy; it did *not* want to go into the doorway. It lunged again, but this time instead of going toward the two men trying to hold it, it went sideways, pulling them both off-balance. Then—this happened really fast—the thing whirled in the other direction, like 180 degrees. Its tail slammed into one of the guys, who went down and lost his hold on the pole. The tail kept going and hit the second guy. He didn't fall, but he also lost his grip on the pole. The thing shook its head and the noose came off.

So now nothing was holding the thing. It started running.

It was running *fast*.

Straight toward Matt and me.

CHAPTER 10

"**R**un!" I said to Matt.

He was already running. The two of us took off along the wall, heading for the canal.

Behind us I heard shouting. I looked back and saw guys running and flashlight beams waving around. Then I saw the thing. It had reached the wall and, unfortunately, turned left, the same direction we were running. It was *really* fast.

"Keep going!" I said to Matt, unnecessarily, because he hadn't even slowed down to look back. We got to the end of the wall and Matt jumped onto the banyan tree like a monkey on steroids. In about two seconds he was on top of the wall.

I tried to follow, but I'm not as good a climber as Matt. My foot got snagged in a tangle of roots, and my sneaker came off. I reached down to grab it. The shouting was getting louder.

"Hurry up!" said Matt. "That thing is coming!"

I didn't dare look. I grabbed my sneaker, stuck it in my shorts pocket, and started climbing again. This time I made it to the top of the wall, where Matt was crouched, waiting for me in the darkness under the branches.

"They caught it," he whispered.

I looked back. They hadn't actually caught the thing, but they had it trapped against the wall, the three guys and the Bevin brothers forming a semicircle around it, shining their flashlights in its eyes. It had its mouth open, looking to bite whoever got close, but you could tell it was confused by the lights. I almost felt sorry for it. One of the guys had the noose pole and they were trying to snag it again.

"Let's go," whispered Matt.

He started climbing down the other side of the wall. I waited until he was down on the dock, then turned and took one last look to where the guys were trying to catch the thing.

That's when a powerful flashlight beam caught me right in the face.

"Hey!" shouted Troy. "Hold it!"

The flashlight started coming my way, fast. I didn't try

to climb down; I basically jumped off the wall, and I almost landed on Matt.

"They saw me," I said.

We grabbed our boards and paddles, ran to the ladder, tossed the boards into the canal, and got on them as fast as we could. We stayed on our knees and paddled with our hands between two of the boats tied to the dock.

The metal door in the wall banged open. There were footsteps running on the dock and flashlight beams flashing around. Matt and I paddled around to the far side of the boat to our right and stopped, holding as still as we could.

"What do we do?" whispered Matt. I could see his face by the dim light from the houses on the other side of the canal. He looked terrified.

"Stay quiet," I whispered.

"Palmer!" It was Troy's voice, from the other side of the dock. "I know you're there."

Nick's voice said, "You sure it was him?"

"*Yes,* I'm sure. He was on top of the wall. Come out, Palmer! Don't make me come get you!"

There were more footsteps on the dock—the Bevins walking around, shining their flashlights, looking for us. Sooner or later they were going to figure out where we were hiding.

Troy said, "He must be on the other side of the boats."

So it was sooner.

"Check that boat," said Troy. "I'll check this one."

I decided our only hope was to start paddling like crazy. The Bevins would see us, but the only way they could catch us was by boat. Of course they *had* a bunch of boats right there. So my plan wasn't really that great. But it was all I could think of at the moment.

"Okay," I whispered to Matt. "We need to get out of here."

"Okay," he whispered.

We crouched on our boards, getting ready to take off.

Then Troy yelled, "Hey!"

Then we heard a hum.

Then the Bevins' flashlight beams were sweeping around the sky.

"There it is!" shouted Nick. "It's a drone!"

Victor must have put new batteries in. From our side of the boat we could see the drone, hovering maybe ten feet over the dock, red light glowing. It rose a little and slowly drifted toward the metal door.

"That thing can take pictures!" said Troy.

The drone drifted slowly over the wall. Like it was luring the Bevins.

"We better get in there," said Troy.

"What about Palmer?" said Nick.

I held my breath.

"We'll get him later," said Troy. "Right now we need to tell them about the drone."

I heard running footsteps, then the sound of the dock gate opening and slamming shut.

I started breathing again.

"Tell Victor thanks," I said to Matt.

"Wyatt says thanks," he said to the Bluetooth. Then, "Victor says we better get out of here."

"No kidding."

Ten seconds later we were up and paddling. Also, thinking. I was thinking, anyway. Mostly I was thinking of questions.

Like, what was that dinosaur thing? Why did they have it? And why were they trying to put it into a hidden underground place?

Why did they even *have* a hidden underground place?

What else did they have in those mounds?

I had a lot more questions, but no answers.

"Wyatt!" Matt was calling from behind me. I stopped paddling so he could catch up.

"What was going on back there?" he said. "What the heck *was* that thing?"

"I have no idea."

"Victor says we need to talk."

"Tell him we'll talk tomorrow. Right now I need to get home."

I started paddling again. I was worried that my parents might have discovered I was gone. But that wasn't my biggest worry. My biggest worry was that the Bevin brothers had seen me. Whatever was going on back there at their house, they obviously wanted to keep it a secret. And now they knew that I knew about it. As if they didn't hate me enough already.

As I paddled, I kept hearing Troy's voice.

We'll get him later.

CHAPTER 11

I got back to my house a little after eleven and climbed back in through my bedroom window. Then I went out to the family room, where my parents, believe it or not, were *still* binge-watching *The Walking Dead*. By that point they must have seen enough splattered zombie brains to cover a basketball court, but they were still into it. I said good night, and they kind of waved good night without taking their eyes off the screen. They never knew I was gone. So at least that was good news.

A minute later I got some bad news, as if I needed any more, when my phone burped. It was my sister, texting me a picture of . . . me. It showed me climbing in through my bedroom window. Taylor's room is next to mine. She must have heard me coming back, leaned out her window, and caught me sneaking in.

I believe I may have mentioned that she can be annoying.

I went into the hall and opened her door. She was sitting on her bed, looking pleased with herself.

"Delete it," I said.

"No," she said.

"Okay, then I'll delete it." I started toward her.

"If you take one more step, I'll scream," she said. "And Mom and Dad will come, and I'll show them the picture, and Mom will kill you."

I stopped, because that is exactly what would happen.

"Come on," I said. "Delete it."

"You could at least ask me nicely," she said. "And you could apologize for just barging into my room."

I took a deep breath and let it out. "Okay," I said. "I'm sorry for barging into your room. *Please* delete the picture."

"No."

Sometimes I hate my sister.

"What do you want?" I said.

"I want to know where you went," she said. In addition to being annoying, she is extremely nosy.

"None of your business," I said.

"All right, then," she said, holding up the phone. "Maybe you'll tell Mom."

"Okay, okay. I went to Matt's house."

"I know that."

"You do?"

"Yeah. I want to know where you and Matt went *after* that. With the paddleboards."

I stared at her. "How do you know about that?"

She swiped her finger across her phone, then showed me the screen. It was another picture; this one was me and Matt getting on our bikes with the paddleboards.

"Where'd you get that?"

"Stella took it," she said. "She saw you guys."

Stella is Matt's little sister. She's also annoying and nosy, so naturally she's one of Taylor's many best friends. They love to get into their older brothers' business. They're like *CSI: Annoying Little Sisters.*

"You guys have nothing better to do than spy on people?"

She ignored that. "Where were you taking the paddleboards?"

I sighed. "The canal."

"Really?" she said, sitting up. She was getting interested, which was bad, because now she'd want to know everything. "Where'd you go?"

"Bay Estates."

"Why?"

"To rescue Matt's ferret."

"*What?* Rescue it from what?"

I realized she was going to keep asking questions, so I gave up and just told her the whole story. To be honest, I kind of wanted to talk about it anyway, even if it had to be with my sister. She listened with her mouth getting wider and wider open, so at the end she looked like that painting where the guy is screaming and his mouth is a big O. When I was done, she said, "Wow."

"Yeah," I said.

"Tell me more about what the giant lizard thing looked like."

So I told her—about the weird head, the saggy skin, the giant tongue, the big claws.

"I think I know what that is," she said. "From science class."

"What is it?"

Instead of answering, she grabbed her iPad and tapped on it for a few seconds. Then she showed me the screen and said, "Look familiar?"

It was a picture of exactly the thing I'd seen at the Bevin house.

"That's it," I said. "What is it?"

"A Komodo dragon."

"Kimono dragon?"

"No," she said, in an annoying I'm-smarter-than-you voice, "a kimono is a robe Japanese people wear. That's a Komodo dragon. It's from Indonesia, and it's an endangered species. I bet it's illegal for them to have it."

My phone burped. It was a text from Matt.

MATT: *u ok?*

ME: *yes u?*

MATT: *my sis saw us*

ME: *i know we need 2 talk*

MATT: *cant now tmrw ok?*

ME: *ok*

"Who was that?" said Taylor.

"Matt."

"What'd he say?"

"That Stella saw us."

Taylor smiled. "You guys aren't very good at this."

"Really? We got Frank back."

"Yeah, but now you're gonna get killed by the Bevin brothers."

I didn't say anything, because she was right.

"So what are you gonna do?" she said.

"About the Bevin brothers?"

"No, the Komodo dragon that they should not have."

"I dunno yet."

"You want me to help?"

I looked at her. I was pretty sure that was the first time she ever said those particular words to me.

"Um, thanks," I said. "I'll let you know. Right now I'm going to bed."

"Okay," she said. Then, out of nowhere, she added, "I'll delete the picture of you sneaking out."

"Thanks," I said. "Good night."

"Good night," she said.

This was absolutely the nicest conversation I'd ever had with my sister. It was so weird it almost made me forget how messed up the rest of the night was.

Almost. But not quite. By the time I was back in my room and in my bed, I was thinking about bad things again. I lay awake for a while in the dark, thinking about scary lizards and scarier people. I finally drifted off to sleep to the familiar sound, drifting in faintly from the TV room, of splattering zombie brains.

CHAPTER 12

"A kimono *dragon*?" said Matt. "It's a *dragon*?"

It was Saturday morning. We—me, Matt, and Victor—were at a Starbucks in Coral Gables. We rode there on our bikes and ordered coffees. Okay, to be honest, we ordered drinks that were basically milk shakes with a little coffee mixed in.

"No it's not a *dragon*," I said. "It's a kind of lizard. And it's Komo*do*, not kimono. A kimono is a Japanese robe."

"If you really saw a Komodo dragon," said Victor, who knows a lot of things about a lot of things, "you're lucky it didn't catch you. Those things can run twenty miles an hour, and they have poison glands in their mouths. They've been known to kill humans."

"Whoa," said Matt. "*We're* humans."

Sometimes "idiot" is too mild a word for Matt.

"What do you mean, *if* we really saw one?" I asked Victor. "We definitely saw it. You didn't see it with the drone?"

"No. I saw a crate, but they must've taken the dragon out when I was changing the batteries."

"So you didn't see the tunnel, either."

"What tunnel?"

"In one of the big grass mounds. It had a hidden door that opened up to a tunnel. That's where they were trying to put the thing."

"I didn't see any opening."

"Well, there is one. I bet all those mounds have tunnels. I wonder what else they have back there."

"At least I got Frank back," said Matt.

"Yeah," I said. "Good for you. But the Bevins know I was there. They were *already* gonna kill me. Now they're gonna kill me multiple times."

"That's one problem," said Victor. "The other one is they have an endangered animal there. If you're right about the mounds, they could have other animals. We need to tell somebody about it."

"Like who?" said Matt. "Our parents?"

"No!" I said. "If I tell my parents, they'll know I snuck out last night, and my mom will *help* the Bevin brothers kill me. Besides, to be honest, I don't think my parents would care about a big lizard. My mom doesn't even like *small* lizards."

This is true. Whenever my mom sees a lizard in our house—which is a lot, because Florida has billions of lizards—she hurries out of the room and tells my dad to get rid of it. About 98 percent of the time the lizard runs under the furniture before my dad can catch it—they're very fast—so my dad ends up pretending he caught it, then pretending to throw it out the front door. Then he yells, "Okay! It's gone!" and my mom comes back into the room, not realizing that the lizard is under the sofa, getting ready to come out and scare her again.

My point is, my mom wouldn't care about rescuing a Komodo dragon.

"I don't think your parents could do anything about it anyway," said Victor.

"So who can?" I said.

"The police."

"Seriously?" I said. "You think we should go to the *police*?"

"They're breaking the law."

I thought about that, slurping my Starbucks.

"Okay," I said, finally. "How do we tell the police?"

"I guess we go to the police station," said Victor. He tapped on his phone. "We're about eight blocks away."

"Suzana's here," said Matt.

I looked up and saw Suzana walking into the Starbucks with three of her girlfriends, all of them hot, but Suzana, as usual, hotter than everybody else. She looked over and saw me looking at her. I made a stupid little wave with my cup. She gave me a little wave back, which—and I know how pathetic this sounds—made me ridiculously happy because she wasn't ignoring me anymore.

Victor, Matt, and I finished our drinks and got up to leave. We walked toward Suzana, who was in line to order coffee.

"Hey," I said. I'm good with words. Mr. Smooth.

"Triple Venti sugar-free, non-fat, no foam, extra caramel, with whip caramel macchiato," she said. Not to me; that was her Starbucks order. To me she said, "Hi."

I wanted to keep the conversation going, but I couldn't think of anything to say except "Hey" again, which would have been stupid. While I was trying to come up with something better, Suzana said to Matt, "So, did you get your little ferret back?"

"Yeah," said Matt. He was going to say more, but Suzana had turned back to me.

"See?" she said. "I told you. They were just kidding."

"Suzana," I said, "they weren't kidding. They're not nice guys. You don't know them."

"I know them better than you do," she said.

"I don't think so."

"I do think so. Because I've actually talked to them."

"Really?" I said. "Well, next time you're talking to them, ask them about what's going on in their backyard."

"What are you talking about?"

I was about to tell her, when Victor grabbed my arm.

"What?" I said, annoyed.

Victor nodded toward the door. I looked that way and saw them walk in.

The Bevin brothers.

Troy was in front. He gave Suzana a big Hollister-model smile featuring numerous spectacularly perfect teeth. "Sorry we're late," he said.

"It's okay," said Suzana. "We just got here."

So this was basically a date.

"He with you?" said Troy, nodding toward me. Behind him, Nick was giving me a look that could have burned a hole in my face.

"No, he was just leaving," said Suzana. "Unless he wants to tell me about your backyard."

Now both Troy and Nick were aiming eyeball lasers at me.

"What about our backyard?" said Troy.

"Yeah, what about it?" said Nick, stepping closer.

"Um," I said, that being the only thing my brain could come up with while it was occupied with trying to prevent me from pooping my pants.

"Um?" said Suzana.

"We have to go," said Victor, pulling me away by my arm.

"We'll finish this later," said Troy.

As Victor pulled me to the door, I heard Suzana say, "What was *that* about?"

"Nothing," said Nick.

I looked back. Troy was staring at me. He mouthed a word, without saying it out loud.

Later.

CHAPTER 13

The police station was a gray stone building that looked kind of like a jail. The lobby was gray and empty except for a policeman at a desk, typing on a computer. A sign in front of him said SGT. KATZEN. He had gray hair and a gray mustache, so he fit in with the overall color scheme. He didn't look excited to see me, Matt, and Victor. But he was polite.

"Can I help you?" he said.

Victor and Matt looked at me. Apparently I had just been elected spokesperson.

"We want to report a crime," I said.

"What kind of crime?"

"We think some guys have a Komodo dragon."

Sgt. Katzen blinked. "They have a dragon?"

"It's not a real dragon," said Matt.

"What is it, then?" said Sgt. Katzen.

"It's a lizard," said Victor.

"A big lizard," I said.

"It's endangered," said Victor.

"Endangered how?" said Sgt. Katzen.

"Just in general," I said. "It's an endangered species."

Sgt. Katzen nodded. "And who are these guys who have this endangered kimono lizard?"

"Not kimono," I said. "Komodo."

"A kimono is a Japanese robe," said Matt.

Sgt. Katzen gave Matt a look that made it clear he had already figured out that Matt was an idiot. "So," he said to me. "Who are these guys who have this endangered Komodo lizard?"

"Their name is Bevin."

All of a sudden Sgt. Katzen looked interested.

"Bevin?" he said. "Frank Bevin?"

"The ones I know are Troy and Nick," I said. "They're high-school students."

"The house is in Bay Estates? Big house?"

"Yes. That's where they have the Komodo dragon."

"So you're telling me," said Sgt. Katzen, "that there's a giant endangered lizard at the Bevin house, and you want to report it as a crime."

"Yes."

Sgt. Katzen looked at me for a few seconds, then said, "Do you know who Frank Bevin is? The man who owns that house?"

"No."

"Mr. Bevin is a very prominent member of this community. *Very* prominent. He's a very respected businessman. He's done a lot of good for a lot of people. A *lot* of good. Mr. Bevin has many, many important friends in this community. Do you understand what I'm telling you?"

I didn't know what to say, so I didn't say anything.

"So," said Sgt. Katzen. "If I start typing your complaint into this"—he pointed at his computer—"I'm going to be opening up a major can of worms. A *major* can of worms. Do you really want to go through with this? Do you understand what you're getting into, here?"

We had no idea what we were getting into. To be honest, I never even understood the expression "can of worms." I mean, seriously, why would anybody put worms in a can in the first place?

Obviously Sgt. Katzen was warning us to not proceed with whatever it was we were doing. But the truth is, we were ninth graders, and we didn't have any idea what we were doing. So, like morons, we all nodded yes.

And Sgt. Katzen, with a big sigh, started typing.

CHAPTER 14

Here's how stupid I am: after we left the police station, I actually started to think that maybe everything was going to be okay. The way I pictured it, the police would go investigate the Bevin house, and they'd find the Komodo dragon and who knows what else. So the Bevins would get into big trouble, maybe even go to jail. But whatever happened to them, they'd have way bigger things to worry about than me. Also, as a side benefit, Suzana would realize that she was wrong, and we'd go back to being friends.

That's the way I pictured it happening.

Sometimes I am a bigger idiot than Matt.

That afternoon I didn't have anything to do, so I went with my family to my sister's soccer game. Taylor is on a U-13 team, which means it's seventh-grade girls. But if you think it's not serious, you don't know anything about Miami soccer parents. Some of them are insane. They act like every game is the World Cup final, only more important. They believe that the referees are all involved in some kind of huge international referee conspiracy to prevent their children from winning. They yell so hard during games that by the end the sidelines are basically drenched with parent spit.

Needless to say my mom is one of the loudest yellers, even though she doesn't know any more about soccer now than she did back when she was yelling at me to KICK THE BALL. In this particular game she was really getting on the referee. He was an older Jamaican guy who had probably refereed a thousand soccer games, but that did not stop my mom from complaining about every call he made against our team. Midway through the second half he called offside against Taylor. When the ref made the call, he happened to be standing directly in front of my mom, but he would have heard her even if he'd been standing in Canada. "OFFSIDE?" she yelled, directly at his butt. "SERIOUSLY? *OFFSIDE??* ARE YOU BLIND *AND* CRAZY?"

The ref turned around slowly and looked right at my mom. Everybody was now totally quiet. My dad buried his face in his hands. Taylor, who for the record had definitely been offside, looked like she wanted to dig a hole in the soccer field and crawl into it.

The ref just stood there for a few seconds, looking at my mom. Everybody was expecting him to give her a warning, or maybe even tell her to leave. Instead, in a polite voice, he said, "Madam, would you mind explaining the offside rule to me?"

"What?" said my mom.

The ref said, "I just thought that since I apparently don't understand it, you could educate me."

My mom, who—like many soccer parents—could no more explain the offside rule than she could operate a nuclear submarine, said nothing. The ref stood there a few more seconds, waiting. Finally he said, "Well, if it comes to you, please don't hesitate to let me know. Meanwhile, I'll try to muddle through as best I can." Then he went back to refereeing.

After that my mom was quiet for nearly ten minutes, which has to be a record. Eventually she started yelling again, which was probably good because otherwise her head would have exploded. But she didn't say another word about offside calls.

The game ended in a tie. I think 95 percent of all soccer games end in a tie. As usual, both sets of parents were unhappy, but the players were fine. Once the game is over, they don't take it as seriously as the parents do.

After the game my mom had a lot to say about the ref. Actually, she had only one thing to say about him, namely that he was an idiot, but she said it about six thousand times. She tried to get the rest of us to agree with her, but we pointed out that, first, he made the right call, and second, all he did was ask her for advice. That was pretty brilliant. I don't know why more refs don't do it.

On the way home we stopped for barbecue at Shorty's, which is this restaurant that has been making barbecue for like sixty years, which makes it basically the most historic thing in Miami. We all love Shorty's, so even my mom was in a pretty good mood by the time we got back home.

The mood changed immediately when we saw what was in front of our house.

Two police cars. And two police officers standing in our driveway.

And both Bevin brothers. They were with a man who looked like an older version of them. Who I guessed was the prominent and respected Mr. Frank Bevin.

"What is THAT about?" said my dad.

I didn't say anything. But based on the hole that suddenly opened up in my stomach, I was pretty sure I knew the answer.

CHAPTER 15

The police cars were blocking our driveway, so Dad parked our car on the street. We all got out and walked to where the police officers and the Bevins were standing. The officers were a youngish, unhappy-looking guy with large muscles, dark hair, and dark eyes, and an older, thicker, red-haired guy who looked like he was in charge. As we walked toward them, I got the feeling everyone was mainly looking at me.

"Is there a problem?" my dad said.

"Are you Mr. Palmer?" said the older cop. He had a little nameplate on his uniform that said DALY.

"Yes," said my dad. "What's this about?"

"This your son?" said Officer Daly, nodding toward me.

"What's this about?" said my mom. "Why are you here?"

"We're investigating a complaint," said Officer Daly.

Both Bevin brothers smiled. That seemed weird. *Why would they be smiling?*

"A complaint against who?" said my mom.

Daly pointed to me and said, "Your son."

Suddenly the hole in my stomach was huge.

"Wait a minute," I said. "You mean a complaint *by* me, right?"

"No," said Daly. "Against you."

The Bevins were really smiling now.

"What complaint?" said my dad. "What's this about?"

"Burglary," said Officer Daly.

What?

"What are you talking about?" said my mom.

"We have reason to believe that last night your son illegally entered the home of Mr. Bevin, here," said Officer Daly, pointing to Frank Bevin.

"That's impossible!" said my mom. "He was home last night. We were home the whole evening, and so was Wyatt."

"Were you in the same room with him the whole evening?" said Daly.

"Well, no, not the whole evening," said my mom. "But he was in his room. Weren't you, Wyatt?"

I didn't say anything.

"Wyatt?" said my mom. "You *were* in your room, right?"

Troy Bevin said, "I saw him in our backyard last night. He knows I did."

"Wyatt," said my dad, "is that true?"

"I want to show you something," said Officer Daly. He went to his police car, reached in, and pulled out a tablet computer. He walked back and tapped on the screen.

"Okay," he said. "This is video taken last night by security cameras at Mr. Bevin's house. Take a look."

My mom and dad moved closer to see the screen. I looked over their shoulders. The video was black-and-white and kind of dark, but we could see the image clearly enough: it was me, climbing over the wall next to the Bevin dock.

"That's the wall around Mr. Bevin's property," said Daly.

My mom and dad looked at me. They were both about to say something when Officer Daly said, "Okay, this is from a camera on the patio."

We looked back at the screen. It showed Matt and me, looking very guilty, scurrying across the patio, then Matt opening the door, then the two of us going inside.

"I believe the other individual is a friend of your son's," said Officer Daly.

"Matt," said my dad, quietly. My mom didn't say anything. That was a very bad sign.

"This next video is from the upstairs hallway."

Now we saw Matt and me looking into one room, then going into another. Then, after an edit, the two of us were coming out, fast, and hurrying toward the stairs.

The video stopped. Officer Daly looked at my parents. They looked at me. Everybody was looking at me. My skin felt hot and my head felt like it was a helium balloon.

My dad said, "Wyatt, what were you doing in that house?"

"I . . . I mean, we . . ." Suddenly I was having trouble talking.

"You *what*?" snapped my dad.

"We were there to get Frank back."

"Who's Frank?" said my dad.

"Matt's ferret."

"His *ferret*?"

"Yes," I said. I pointed to the Bevin brothers. "They took Frank. They were going to feed him to Roxy."

"Roxy?" said Officer Daly.

"Roxy's a big snake," I said.

"So you're telling me," said Officer Daly, "that you climbed the wall and entered the Bevin house to rescue a ferret from a snake."

"Yes," I said.

The Bevin brothers snickered. Officer Daly was smiling a little.

"I know it sounds stupid," I said. "But it's the truth."

"Did you get . . . whatsitsname? Fred?" said Officer Daly.

"It's Frank," I said. "Yes. We found him in Nick's room, next to the snake cage."

"So you had the ferret when you left the room?" said Officer Daly.

"Yes," I said. "Matt did."

"So why don't I see it in the video?"

"Because Matt put it in his hoodie pocket."

"I see," said Officer Daly, who clearly didn't believe me.

"Okay, listen," I said. "Never mind the ferret. The important thing is, while we were there, we saw something in the backyard."

Suddenly the Bevins weren't snickering. The dad gave me a hard look.

Officer Daly said, "What did you see in the backyard?"

"A Komodo dragon. Some men brought it in a boat."

"What the heck is a kimono dragon?" said my mom.

"It's a Komodo dragon," said Taylor. "A kimono is a Japanese robe."

"Thank you, Miss Wikipedia," said my mom. "So what the heck is a Komodo dragon?"

"It's a huge lizard," I said. "Like the size of an alligator. It's an endangered species. They're not supposed to have it."

My parents were looking at me like I was insane.

"We saw it!" I said. "They have a tunnel in their backyard! We saw it! I swear!"

"So you told Sgt. Katzen this morning," said Officer Daly. To my parents, he said, "Your son and his friend filed a police complaint about this against the Bevins."

"You filed a complaint with the *police*?" my dad said.

"Dad," I said, "it's *true*. There was a Komodo—"

"We investigated the complaint," interrupted Officer Daly.

"You did?" I said.

"Actually, Officer Morales did." Officer Daly nodded toward the younger police officer, who was looking at me unhappily. "Officer Morales checked out the backyard of the Bevin house, with the full cooperation of Mr. Bevin. Officer Morales, what did you find in the backyard?"

"A backyard," said Officer Morales.

"No dragon?"

"No dragon."

"That's because it's underground!" I said. "They're hiding it under one of those mounds! There's a tunnel!"

Everybody was staring at me.

"Officer Morales," said Officer Daly, "did you see a tunnel in Mr. Bevin's backyard?"

"I did not."

"It's hidden!" I said. "It has a secret entrance! I saw it! You need to go back and look again! I'll show you where it is!"

Officer Daly sighed. "So that's your story? That's why you claim you were at Mr. Bevin's house?"

"Yes! It's the truth!"

"You're sure there's not some *other* reason?"

"What are you talking about?"

"I'm talking about something that was missing from Nick Bevin's room, the room you and your friend went into."

"What's missing?" I said.

"A watch. An Apple watch."

"We didn't take his watch!"

Nick spoke up. "It's the forty-two millimeter model. It's gone."

My mom gasped. She grabbed my arm. "Did you take his watch?"

"No!" I said. "We just went to get Frank back!"

"You stole my watch," said Nick. "And then Troy saw you climbing the wall. You knew we'd figure out it was you who took the watch. So you made up this stupid story about some endangered lizard as a distraction, to get us in trouble."

"That's not true!" I said. "We saw the dragon!"

Even to me, that sounded kind of weird.

Officer Daly held up his hand to quiet me and Nick. He turned to my parents and said, "Look, I'd like to clear this up as quickly as possible."

"So would we," said my dad.

"So what I'm asking," said Officer Daly, "is if you'd give me permission to take a look around your son's room."

Dad looked at me.

"Go ahead," I said. "I don't have his watch."

"All right, then," said Officer Daly. "Mr. Bevin, why don't you and your sons stay out here with Officer Morales. I'll go inside with the Palmers."

We trudged up the walkway to our house. My dad unlocked the front door and we went inside, where we were joyfully attacked by our large hairy dog, Csonka, who as my dad likes to say is a cross between a Labrador retriever and an aircraft carrier. Csonka is always very sad when we leave the house. And whenever we come back, even if we were only gone five minutes, Csonka has to demonstrate, by intensive licking, how thrilled he is to have us home again. He's always especially thrilled if we bring somebody new, like Officer Daly. After he licked Officer Daly hello, he sprinted off to get his favorite toy, which is a stuffed animal that was originally supposed to look like a hedgehog, although after years of being slobbered on by Csonka it's really just a filthy disgusting wad of fur. It has a squeaker in it, which amazingly still works. Csonka came racing back with his hedgehog, squeaking it like crazy and prancing around Officer Daly, trying to get Officer Daly to try to take it away, which is Csonka's favorite game. He thinks everybody wants his hedgehog as much as he does.

But Officer Daly didn't want the hedgehog. Nobody was in the mood to play with Csonka. So he ended up just standing there, squeaking a little sadly, as we all walked past and went down the hall to my bedroom.

I wasn't nervous. I was upset about the Bevins calling the police on me, but I wasn't worried about Officer Daly searching my room, because I knew I didn't have the watch.

We stopped outside my door.

"This is his room," said my dad.

Officer Daly opened the door and went in. My parents, Taylor, and I stood in the hall, watching. Behind us stood Csonka, emitting the occasional squeak in case anybody wanted to play.

Officer Daly was methodical, going around the room clockwise, starting near the door. He looked in my closet, checked the shelves, then moved to my desk and went through the drawers. He walked by the window to my bed. He knelt and looked under the bed, then lifted the mattress enough to look under it. Then he picked up the two pillows.

Then he stopped and looked.

There, on the bed, was the watch.

CHAPTER 16

"Ohmigod," said my mom.

My dad was staring at me.

Officer Daly reached down and picked up the watch.

"I did *not* put that there," I said. "I swear."

"Then how did it get there?" said Officer Daly.

"I don't *know*," I said. "I swear I didn't—"

"The window," said Taylor.

Everybody looked at her. "Did you lock it when you came in last night?" she said.

I thought about it. I left it unlocked when I snuck out so I could sneak back in. I didn't remember locking it when I got home. "No," I said. "I don't think so."

Taylor looked at Officer Daly. "So that's how they did

it. They came in through the window while we were at the soccer game. They had lots of time."

"Who's 'they'?" said Officer Daly.

"The Bevins."

"You think they planted the watch here?"

"They must have!" I said.

"Why would they do that?"

"They want to frame me!" I said.

"But why?"

"Because I saw the Komodo dragon at their house! They want to get me out of the way!"

"You mean the Komodo dragon that Officer Morales didn't find when he went over there?"

"But it's there! Matt saw it too!"

Officer Daly sighed. "Son, you're just making it worse for yourself, here. Mr. Bevin is a reasonable man. If you just admit what you did . . ."

"But I didn't do it!" I said. "I swear I didn't! I'm not a thief! Mom, Dad, don't you believe me?"

I looked at them both.

Mom was crying.

Dad was looking away.

They didn't believe me.

"Mr. and Mrs. Palmer," said Officer Daly, "I need to take your son to the police station."

CHAPTER 17

The good news was, I didn't have to go to jail. Neither did Matt, who was also picked up at his house and taken down to the police station. We got a long lecture from Officer Daly about what *could* happen to us. He mentioned the word "prison" maybe fifteen times. Every time, my mom made a moaning sound.

The worst part was the Bevin brothers, who sat with their father during the lecture, looking at me and Matt, but mainly me. They tried to look serious, but I could see in their eyes that they were totally loving watching us get reamed out.

After the reaming, Officer Daly told us that the great and

powerful Mr. Frank Bevin had decided, very generously, not to press charges. My dad shook Frank's hand and thanked him like fifty times; I thought my mom was going to kiss him. Matt's parents also went on and on about how grateful they were. Frank Bevin said he was a parent himself, and he understood that boys will be boys and kids sometimes did stupid things, but it shouldn't ruin their lives. Then he looked at Matt and me and said there was one condition, which was that he did not want us to come on his property again. My parents and Matt's parents said absolutely, we would never come anywhere near the Bevin house. My mom assured Frank that if I got caught on his property, I wouldn't have to worry about going to prison, because she, personally, would kill me.

I wasn't 100 percent sure she was exaggerating.

Anyway, I was relieved that I wasn't going to prison. But something bothered me. Why did Frank Bevin make such a big deal about us not going to his house? I didn't believe he really thought we would go back there and try to steal stuff. I believed it had to do with whatever was going on in his backyard. The look he shot at Matt and me was not a friendly, forgiving look. It was a mean look, and it said *stay away*.

Which I definitely planned to do.

We walked out of the police station with Matt's family. Matt and I stood for a few minutes on the sidewalk listening to the two sets of parents discuss what a pair of disrespectful idiots we were and how long they planned to ground us. They didn't decide on a definite time period, but they agreed it would be many days. Possibly even months. Possibly *years*. Possibly they would decide to confine us to our rooms for the rest of our lives. When we died the hearse would carry us directly from our rooms to the cemetery. Our tombstones would say PERMANENTLY GROUNDED.

So maybe we would have been better off with jail.

While we were standing on the sidewalk, the three Bevins came out of the station. My parents and Matt's parents decided that they had to thank Frank Bevin *again* for being so generous and forgiving and blah blah blah.

While that was going on, Nick and Troy drifted over to where I was standing. They both had big smiles on their faces. Nick stuck out his hand to shake mine. "No hard feelings, right, Palmer?"

Like an idiot, I stuck my hand out. Nick took it and started squeezing, hard. My hand felt like a truck was driving over it. I tried to pull it away, but Nick just squeezed harder, still smiling. I didn't want to give him the satisfaction of hearing me whimper, but I did make kind of a high-pitched noise, and I could feel tears in my eyes. Of course my parents didn't notice any of this because they were too busy kissing the wonderful generous butt of Mr. Frank Bevin.

Finally, just when I thought all the bones in my hand were going to crack, Nick let go.

"See you in school, Palmer," he said.

I didn't say anything. I was rubbing my right hand with my left. Trying to get the pain out.

Troy leaned over and—just loud enough for me to hear but nobody else—said, "You really should keep your bedroom window locked."

Then the Bevins got into Frank's brand-new black Mercedes Maybach S600, which cost like $200,000, and drove smoothly away. I rode home with my family in my dad's eight-year-old Toyota Camry, listening to my mom tell me, in great detail, all the ways my behavior was unacceptable.

Other than that it was a fun Saturday.

CHAPTER 18

When we got home my parents told me to go straight to my room. At least they didn't take away my phone. So I texted with Matt, who was also stuck in his room. Mainly we texted about how much the situation sucked, especially the fact that our own parents thought we were thieves.

During this conversation Matt actually had a good idea, which was that maybe Victor could fly his drone over the Bevin backyard to get some video proof that we were telling the truth. So we texted Victor and told him what was going on, and he said that after it got dark, he'd go out on the patio to watch the Bevin house and see if he could figure out a good time to fly the drone across the canal. He said he'd connect with us on MultiFacet, which was this app he had on his phone that would let him stream video from the drone so we could watch. Victor is very tech-y.

While I was sitting around my room waiting for it to get dark, Taylor knocked on my door.

"What," I said.

She opened the door and peeked in. "Can I talk to you?"

"About what? How I'm grounded forever?" I really didn't feel like hearing her mock me, which is what I figured she wanted to do.

"No," she said, stepping into my room and closing the door. "I wanted to help you."

"Help me what?"

"Prove those people have a Komodo dragon. I think it's horrible that they have that poor animal in captivity."

"Okay," I said, "but that poor animal is huge, and it looked like it wanted to eat somebody."

"That's because it was scared."

"Well that makes two of us."

"Anyway, I want to help."

"How?"

"Marissa lives in Bay Estates."

Marissa is another one of Taylor's best friends. She has like ten of them.

"So?"

"So I could go to Marissa's house, and I could walk over to the Bevins' and try to get a picture of the Komodo dragon."

I held up my hand. "Taylor, no. You can't do that."

"Why not?"

"Because these are bad guys."

"I'm not afraid of them."

"Well, you should be. They're really bad, and they're not going to let you just walk in and take pictures."

"They won't even notice me. I'll just be some harmless little girl around the neighborhood."

"Taylor, no. It's too dangerous."

"So you're just gonna let them get away with this?"

"I didn't say that."

"Do you have a plan?"

"Kind of."

That perked her up. "Really? What is it?"

I sighed, because there was no way she was going to leave until she knew everything. So I told her about Victor's drone.

"I like it," she said. "Text me when we're ready to start."

"We?" I said.

"Yeah, *we*," she said, on her way out the door.

So as if the day wasn't already weird enough, now I was Plan Buddies with my sister, even though, technically, we hated each other.

114

I spent an hour or so watching random stuff on Netflix without really seeing it. It got dark out. I kept staring at my phone. Finally it made a *boop*ing sound, and there was Victor in a box on the screen, holding his drone. He had a Bluetooth thing in his ear. There were two smaller boxes on the bottom of the screen, one with Matt in it, and one with me.

"Can you guys see me?" said Victor.

Matt and I said we could. My door opened and Taylor came in. She must have been lurking outside listening. She sat on the bed next to me.

"Hi, Victor; hi, Matt," she said.

"Why is *she* there?" said Matt.

"Never mind," I said.

"Okay, listen," said Victor. "A boat just pulled up to the Bevins' dock, so I'm gonna launch the drone. I'm changing the video feed now so we can watch the drone camera on our phones. Let me know if it's working." The screen went black for a few seconds, and then we were seeing Victor's sneakers on the patio, in the weird green color you see on night-vision cameras.

"It's working," I said. "I can see your feet."

"Me too," said Matt.

"Okay," said Victor. "Here goes."

He set the drone down, so now we were seeing a super-close-up view of a patio brick. Then he turned on the drone and it started to rise. We saw more bricks, and then we saw Victor, with green skin, looking up at the drone and holding the remote controller. He got smaller as the drone rose, then disappeared off the edge of the screen as it moved out over the canal. For ten seconds or so we mainly saw blackness while the drone crossed the canal. I shivered a little, remembering what it was like to paddle on that dark water at night.

Then the drone was over the Bevins' dock, and we could see boats tied up. The metal door in the wall was open. The drone slowed down and went over the wall. I was leaning over my phone now, staring hard at the screen, trying to make sense of the greenish blobs below.

"There they are," said Victor.

I saw them. Moving green people-shapes on the edge of the screen, surrounding a squarish thing.

"It looks like another crate," I said. "But it's smaller than the other one."

The drone was right over them now. They were moving the crate along the walkway, toward the house.

"I'm going lower," said Victor.

The drone started down slowly. I counted four people-shapes around the crate. I kind of thought I could make out the Bevin brothers down there, but I wasn't sure.

"Careful," I said to Victor. I was almost whispering, even though there was no way the shapes could hear me.

116

The drone got lower. The shapes had stopped now. It looked like they were next to one of the mounds.

The drone dropped a little lower. One of the shapes turned on a flashlight—it was a really bright greenish-white on the screen—and shined it sideways, and I could see I was right—they were next to one of the weird backyard mounds. Another shape moved toward the mound.

"Okay," I said, "I think maybe they're about to open a door."

Now I was staring at my phone screen so hard my eyes hurt. The shape leaned over and reached toward the mound. This was it; they were going to open the door, and then we'd see them transfer whatever was in the crate.

"Get ready to record this," I said.

"Okay," said Victor.

Then suddenly the flashlight swung away from the mound and pointed up, straight at the drone. The light made the screen flare almost totally white.

"Get it out of there!" I said.

Then the screen went black.

"What happened?" That was Matt's voice.

"Victor?" I said. "You there?"

"Hang on," said Victor. The screen was still black. About a minute went by. Then the screen flickered and Victor's face appeared.

"You guys there?" he said.

"Yeah," said Matt.

I said, "What happened?"

"I think they shot the drone," said Victor.

"What?"

"I heard a popping sound across the canal, and the camera went out. I've been trying to make the drone fly back this way, but I don't see or hear it. I think they shot it down."

"Like with a gun?" said Matt.

"Yeah," said Victor. "Like with a gun."

"Wow," said Taylor. She looked at me. "They *are* bad guys."

"That thing was expensive," said Victor. "I don't know how I'm going to explain this to my parents."

"Can't you tell them the truth?" said Matt.

"Not really," said Victor. "I'm not supposed to use it to spy on neighbors. They were really clear about that when I got it. Plus, I can't *prove* the Bevins shot it."

"Victor," I said, "do you think the Bevins know where the drone came from?"

"I don't think so," he said. "I mean, I guess they could figure out it was being controlled by somebody nearby. But it doesn't have my name on it."

Everybody was quiet for a few seconds, then Matt said, "So what do we do now?"

Victor said, "I'm going to try to figure out what to tell my parents. That thing was *really* expensive."

"I mean," said Matt, "what are we going to do about the Bevins?"

"Maybe we should just leave the Bevins alone," said Victor.

"Yeah," I said. "We're in enough trouble as it is."

"Seriously?" said Taylor. "You're just going to let them get away with it? Framing you for stealing? Smuggling endangered animals, and whatever else they're up to over there? You're not going to try to stop them?"

"We tried to stop them," I said. "They shot down the drone. They have *guns,* Taylor."

"So call the police."

"We did that once already, remember?" I said. "The police think the Bevins are the good guys and we're the criminals."

Everybody was quiet again. Then Matt said, "This totally sucks."

Everybody agreed with that, even Taylor.

We sat around a little longer, staring at each other on our screens, but nobody had any brilliant ideas. So we all said good night and hung up. Taylor went back to her room. I locked my window, wishing I'd done that the night before, and went to bed.

I was tired, but I had a hard time falling asleep, and when

I finally did I had a dream where I was being chased by a Komodo dragon, except it could talk, and its voice sounded like Principal Arlene "The Stinger" Metzinger, telling me that when she caught up with me she was going to put me in detention forever. I was in a hallway, which I think was in Coral Cove High, and my legs felt super-heavy, so no matter how hard I tried to run, I could barely move. I could hear the Komodo Stinger getting closer and closer because its claws were making a clicking sound on the floor, like *click-click-click-click*. The clicking was getting louder and louder, *CLICK-CLICK-CLICK-CLICK*, and my legs were getting heavier and heavier, and I knew the Komodo Stinger was going to catch me, and then . . .

. . . and then I woke up, covered with sweat. I looked at my phone. It was 3:14 a.m. I realized I had thrown my blanket, sheet, and pillow on the floor.

Then I realized something else.

I could still hear the clicking.

Except it wasn't really clicking. It was more like tapping. *Tap-tap-tap-tap.* And it was coming from close by.

Very close by.

Somebody was tapping on my bedroom window.

Tap-tap-tap-tap.

The first thing I thought was: *Bevin brothers.*

They had already come through my bedroom window

once. I didn't know why they would come back, but I figured it wouldn't be to bring me home-baked cookies.

From my bed, I couldn't see out the window. My room was dark, so whoever was tapping couldn't see in, either.

Tap-tap-tap-tap.

For a few seconds I just lay in bed, sweating, hoping whoever it was would just go away.

Tap-tap-tap-tap.

They weren't going away.

I sat up and put my feet on the floor. I decided I'd go to the door, open it quickly, and leave. I wasn't sure what I'd do after that. Probably tell my parents. At the moment I just wanted to get away from whoever was out there. I stood and took a couple of shuffling steps toward the door, my hand reaching out for it in the darkness.

Tap-tap-tap-tap.

I admit this is pathetic, but I was afraid to look toward the window. I was actually squinting, like a little kid who thinks that if he closes his eyes, nobody can see him.

I felt around until I found the doorknob. I turned it and opened the door. There was a light on in the hallway, so now whoever was outside could see me. Suddenly the tapping stopped, and I heard a smacking sound, like a hand slapping the window. I didn't want to look, but I couldn't help myself. I turned toward the window. I was expecting to see a face. Instead, I saw a piece of notebook paper pressed against the glass. On it, handwritten in big black letters, were these words:

I KNOW WHAT THEY ARE DOING.
HELP ME STOP THEM.

CHAPTER 19

I stared at the sign for a second, then stepped into the hall and closed the door. I stared at the door, trying to decide what to do.

Taylor's door opened. She poked her head out.

"Somebody's outside your window," she whispered.

"I know," I said.

"Who is it?"

"I don't know. But they're holding up a note that says they know what the Bevins are doing."

"Really?" She came out into the hall. Csonka, who had

been sleeping in the living room, also wandered in, to see what was going on.

"I think that's what they mean. The note says 'I know what they are doing. Help me stop them.'"

"Wow. Who could it be?"

"I have no idea."

"So let's find out."

Before I could say anything, Taylor opened the door and went into my room, followed by Csonka. So unless I wanted to stand in the hall like a total coward, I had to follow my dog and my annoyingly brave little sister.

I looked at the window. The note was gone, but I could see a dark shape out there. I couldn't see the face.

"Can you tell who that is?" said Taylor.

"No."

"Only one way to find out." She went to the window, unlocked it, and slid it open.

"Who's there?" she said.

"Me," said the shape, stepping forward and poking his head in. He was a youngish guy, looked like maybe in his mid-twenties. He had longish hair.

"Hi," he said. "Mind if I come in?"

"Sure," said Taylor.

"Wait a minute," I said, but he was already climbing into my room. He was tall and skinny, wearing shorts with a T-shirt that said SNOT HOUSE. Csonka, who is the worst watchdog ever, went right over and starting licking him. Csonka would lick Godzilla.

"Hey there, boy," said the guy, rubbing Csonka's head.

"What's Snot House?" said Taylor. As if that was the big question on everybody's mind at the moment.

"A band," said the guy. "They're really good."

"Okay, that's terrific," I said. "Now who are you and why are you here?"

"My name's Jon Aibel," he said. "I'm here to see you. You're Wyatt Palmer, right?"

"Yes. But who are—"

"And you told the police you saw a Komodo dragon in Frank Bevin's backyard?"

"How do you know that?"

"I have a police source. So it's true?"

"It's true. There's a Komodo dragon back there. But nobody believes me."

"I believe you."

"You do?"

"Yup. What else did you see?"

"What do you mean?"

"Did you see any other unusual animals?"

"We saw a python inside the house."

"No, in the backyard. Did you see any other animals there?"

125

"Okay, hold it. Before I answer any more of your questions, who *are* you? Why are you tapping on my window at three a.m.?"

"Fair enough," he said. "I guess I owe you an explanation."

"Yeah."

"Okay. Believe it or not, until a month ago, I worked for the United States government. I was with the Fish and Wildlife Service. You know what they do?"

"They deal with fish," said Taylor. "And wildlife."

"Ignore her," I said. "She thinks she's clever."

Jon Aibel smiled at Taylor, who blushed, which meant she thought he was cute. I felt a little sorry for him.

"Anyway," he continued, "among other things, Fish and Wildlife enforces the Endangered Species Act. You know what that is, right?"

Taylor and I nodded.

"Okay," he said. "So smuggling rare animals is a huge business worldwide. I'm talking literally billions of dollars. And Miami is right in the middle of it. The Miami airport has more incoming animals than any other airport in the country, and a lot of those animals aren't supposed to be here. Sometimes they're in big shipments from professional smugglers, going to shady dealers here. Sometimes it's some amateur nimrod who went to the Amazon rain forest and came home with an iguana stuffed down his pants."

"His *pants?*" said Taylor.

"You would not believe what people put in their pants. I've seen snapping turtles."

"Ouch," I said.

"Exactly. So anyway, a lot of animals come to Miami illegally, and not just through the airport. They come by truck, by car, by boat, whatever, and Fish and Wildlife agents try to stop them. Some of these are special agents. Sometimes they work in plain clothes and go undercover, infiltrate smuggling operations, stuff like that. I was one of those agents."

"Wow," said Taylor. She was now officially in love.

"So anyway, there was this dealer in Miami, specializing in herps, and—"

"What's herps?" I said.

"It's slang for herpetofauna. Reptiles and amphibians. Collectors call them 'herps' for short."

"Cool," said Taylor, unnecessarily. He smiled at her, which is of course why she said it.

"So anyway," he said, "we suspected this dealer was shady, so I started hanging around, pretending to be a rich collector interested in rare herps. Do you know what a black mamba is?"

We shook our heads.

"It's a venomous African snake. It's big—it can get to ten feet, even longer. It's also aggressive, which means trouble because it's one of the fastest snakes in the world, and one of

127

the most deadly. Its venom is extremely toxic. Two drops can kill you. The venom attacks your nervous system, and if you don't get treatment fast, you will die a very painful, unpleasant death. In other words, this is one of the most dangerous animals on the planet. So naturally there are people who want one as a pet."

"Why?" I said.

"Because there's a certain kind of guy—it's almost always a guy—who wants to possess deadly animals. The deadlier the better. Every now and then one of these guys gets himself or somebody else killed, but that just makes it more exciting for the rest of them. So anyway, I'm hanging around this herps dealer, pretending to be a rich amateur collector who wants his own personal black mamba. You're not allowed to possess one in this country unless you're putting it in a legitimate zoo, or you're a researcher, somebody with the right qualifications and training. But I let it be known that I'd pay a lot of money to get a mamba, no questions asked."

"So did they sell you one?" I asked.

"Not the dealer. He said he didn't have one, although I think he was just being careful because he didn't know me. But there was this guy named Luis who was always hanging around there, heard I was in the market, and said maybe he could help me out. So I met him at a bar and bought him a few drinks, which turned him into quite a talker. Long story short, he sometimes worked for these high-end smugglers who specialized in rare and dangerous animals, and they happened to be bringing in some black mambas for a big client they had. He said maybe, for the right price, he could get one for me. I think he was planning to steal one from the smugglers and sell it to me, to make some money on the side. So I said sure, get me one. I wasn't really after Luis. I was after the bigger guys. I figured I could get to them through Luis."

"So did you?" said Taylor.

He looked at her, but this time he didn't smile. "We were supposed to meet in Coconut Grove. He was going to give me the snake, and I'd give him the money. But he never showed up. I figured he got cold feet. But two days after that, some boaters found a body floating in Biscayne Bay, near Matheson Hammock. Guess who."

"It was Luis?" said Taylor.

He nodded. "At first the police thought it was an accidental drowning. But when I found out about it, I asked them to do a blood toxicology test. Guess what they found."

"Black mamba venom," I said.

"Bingo."

"So what do you think happened?"

"At first I thought maybe he messed up handling it and it bit him. But a couple of things bothered me about that. One was: This guy was experienced with snakes. He'd be very careful with a mamba. Another thing was: Why was he in the water? If you get bitten by a snake, even if you're on a boat, you don't jump overboard. But the weirdest thing was *where* he was bitten."

"Where?" I said.

"On the back of his head."

"Whoa," I said. "That's not an accident."

"No. It was just above his neck, where his hair would cover the puncture marks. Which is why nobody saw them when they fished him out of the bay. Somehow the guys he worked for must have found out he was going to steal the snake. I think they held him down, had the snake bite him, and threw him overboard. He'd try to swim, but the venom would be attacking his nervous system. He had no chance."

"Wow," I said.

"Yeah," he said. "These are very bad guys."

"So what did you do?" said Taylor. "Did you arrest them?"

"At first, Luis didn't give me any names. I think he wanted to make sure I couldn't bypass him and buy direct from them. But he did tell me some things, back when we were at the bar. He told me what kinds of animals they'd been bringing in for this big client. And after a couple of drinks, he let slip the client's name. See if you can guess."

"Frank Bevin," I said.

"Bingo."

CHAPTER

20

"**S**o that's *good*, right?" I said. "Now you can arrest the Bevins, or at least investigate them."

Jon Aibel smiled, but it was not a happy smile. "That's what I thought," he said. "I went straight to my superiors, told them what I knew. I thought we'd get a warrant and be raiding the Bevin property within hours. I thought I'd be a hero, maybe get a promotion." He shook his head. "That's not what happened."

"What happened?" I said.

"My boss told me to stop investigating."

"Why?"

"He didn't say. I got the feeling that the order came from way above him."

"But there was a dead guy!" said Taylor.

"That's what I said. My boss said that was a police matter and I should stay out of it."

"But you knew *why* he was dead!" I said. "You knew about the smuggling!"

"I pointed that out, and my boss said that everything was under control—whatever that was supposed to mean—and that I was absolutely under strict orders to stay away from that case."

"So did you?" I asked.

"For a couple of days. But as far as I could tell, nothing was happening. It was driving me crazy. I mean, a guy was dead, and I felt at least partly responsible. So I went to the police on my own. I told them everything I knew. Guess what happened."

"What?"

"Instead of investigating, the police went straight to my bosses, and I got suspended from Fish and Wildlife. For insubordination."

"Seriously?"

"Yup. And I was told that if I talked to anybody else about this, I'd lose my job permanently *and* get arrested for interfering with an investigation. Except as far as I can tell there *is* no investigation."

"But why not?"

"It seems that Frank Bevin is untouchable. He's a rich and powerful man, and he has powerful friends, and they're not going to let anything happen to him. He can do whatever he wants in his compound, even if what he wants to do is collect the most lethal animals on earth in the backyard of a residential neighborhood. If something goes wrong over there, innocent people will be in danger."

"You mean like if the mamba snakes get out?" said Taylor.

"Yup. Or the Komodo dragon. Or the deathstalker scorpions."

"The *what* scorpions?"

"Deathstalker. They're from North Africa and the Middle East, and they're as nasty as they sound. You do *not* want to get stung by one."

"No," I agreed.

"Well, according to my late friend Luis, Frank Bevin brought in dozens of them. He also has a bunch of poison dart frogs and Brazilian wandering spiders, both of which are deadly. And then there's something else he got, something truly weird and scary."

"Wait," I said. "Weirder and scarier than deathstalker scorpions?"

"Yup. I thought I knew every kind of animal that ever got smuggled into this town, but I never heard of this. According-ing to Luis, one night the smugglers hired him for a boat transport, only this time they used a bigger boat than usual. They went out into the Gulf Stream and met a freighter, but instead of an animal crate, a big aluminum container was loaded onto their boat. They headed back toward Miami and got to the Bevin house at around two a.m. They had a major hassle getting the container inside the wall. It just barely fit through the gate. By now Luis was really curious about what was inside there. So finally he asked one of the head guys. When the guy told him, Luis could barely believe it."

"What was it?" I said.

"Siafu."

"Wow," said Taylor.

I looked at her. "You know what that is?"

"No," she admitted.

I looked at Jon Aibel. "What's a siafu?"

"It's a kind of ant."

"The container is full of *ants*?"

"Yes. African ants. They're also called driver ants or safari ants."

"What's so scary about an ant?" said Taylor.

"Well, if there's just *one*, it's not that scary, although they do have extremely powerful jaws, so even one can give you a pretty painful bite. But the thing about siafu is, there's never just one. They form the biggest ant colonies in the world—sometimes twenty million ants. *Twenty million.* And they work together, so they're like one big creature that has millions of jaws. They're swarm raiders, which means they go out and hunt for food in a huge mass, like a river of ants. They eat pretty much any animal in their path. Usually that's other insects, earthworms, rodents, stuff like that. But they've been known to kill cattle."

"You mean like a *cow*?" said Taylor. "Ants can kill a *cow*?"

"It happens, especially if the cow has been tied up and can't run. Goats and dogs, too. The ants look for openings, so they go into the animal's mouth and nose, thousands and thousands of them, filling up the airways so the animal can't breathe. It dies from asphyxiation, and then the ants tear it apart."

"Ew," said Taylor.

"Can they kill people?" I said.

"If you can walk, you can get away from them," he said. "If you can't walk—say you broke a leg and you're lying on the ground, or for some reason you're unconscious, if the

siafu get to you . . ." He shook his head. "That's a very, very unpleasant way to die."

For a few seconds nobody said anything. Then I said, "So you're saying that's what was in the container? Ants?"

He nodded. "Apparently."

"But how is that even possible? How do you get twenty million ants into a box?"

"I've thought about that. I think the way they must have done it is by putting on hazmat suits and attacking a siafu hill with earthmoving equipment while the colony was inside. If they were organized and moved fast, they could do it before the colony could organize and move. Scoop them up in the dirt, dump them in the container, toss some meat in there for food, close the container up, and seal it tight. I think it could be done. I mean, obviously, it *was* done. The question is, *why?*"

"You already said why," said Taylor. "Bevin is collecting dangerous animals."

"Yeah, but here's the thing. Collectors like to be able to look at their animals, to watch them move, and especially to watch them eat. They keep them in cages or display cases so they can see them. You can't do that with a sealed container. You'd have to be crazy to even open it. But at some point, they *have* to open it, or the ants will starve to death in there. So why did Frank Bevin go to all that trouble to bring them here from Africa? And why is he assembling the zoo from hell in his backyard? It's driving me crazy, especially that I can't do anything about it, can't even *talk* to anybody about it without getting arrested. So when I heard about you and the Komodo dragon . . ."

"How did you hear about that?" I said.

"Like I said, I have a police source, a guy who doesn't like the way the higher-ups are rolling over for Bevin. He told me about you and your friend Matt getting picked up, and he told me where you lived. I waited until late to come see you because we'd both get in trouble if anybody found out I was here. I hope that's okay."

"Totally okay," said Taylor. She actually batted her eyelashes at him.

"Yeah, it's okay," I said. "But why are you here? I mean, what do you want from me?"

He rubbed his chin. "I'm not sure. Partly I just wanted to confirm that I'm not crazy about what's going on over there. But I guess I was also hoping that you'd tell me something that would help me understand *why* it's going on, and what I can do to stop it. Because whatever it is, it can't be good."

"But you can't do anything about it," I said. "You'll get arrested."

"I have to try," he said. "I already feel responsible for one guy dying. I don't want to be responsible for more."

"But it's not *your* fault, what the Bevins do."

He looked at me. "I can't just do nothing."

"Well," said Taylor, "we can't do nothing, either. We can help."

"We can?" I said.

"Yes," she said. "We can help you, Mr. Aibel."

He smiled. "Call me Jon."

"Okay, Jon," she said, batting her eyelashes so hard she could have strained an eyelid muscle.

"The thing is," he said, "at this point, I have no idea what *I* can do, and while I appreciate the offer of help . . ." He looked at Taylor and me, and he didn't finish the sentence, but what he obviously was thinking was, *I don't see how I'm going to get much help from a ninth-grade boy who's permanently grounded and a seventh-grade girl who's acting like I'm her favorite boy band.*

"Anyway," he said, finally, "I really do appreciate it. But it's going to be getting light soon. I better take off."

"Okay," I said.

"Okay," said Taylor, in a much sadder voice.

"How about we exchange phone numbers, in case we need to get in touch," he said.

So we exchanged numbers. Jon said good-bye, climbed out the window, and was gone.

As soon as the window closed, Taylor said, "He's *really* cute."

"Great," I said.

"We have to help him."

"Because he's cute?"

"No, because he needs our help. . . . Also because he's cute."

"How are we supposed to help him?"

"I don't know. But we have to think of something."

"Taylor, I'm already in huge trouble. I can't—"

"Okay, *don't*," she said, standing up. "*Don't* help him. Just sit around and feel sorry for yourself, and when something terrible happens, just tell yourself there was nothing you could do."

I didn't have anything to say to that.

She turned around and walked out.

I tried to sleep, but every time I drifted off, the Komodo dragon with Principal Metzinger's voice was chasing me. I would wake up, sweating, and then I'd drift back to sleep, and there would be the Principal Metzinger dragon again. And I couldn't get away from the feeling that sooner or later, no matter how hard I tried to run, it was going to catch me.

CHAPTER 21

You know how sometimes, when you're waking up from a bad dream, it still seems real, and then you realize it was just a dream and you feel relieved?

I had the opposite experience Sunday morning. I woke up thinking, *Whoa, thank goodness I'm not being chased by a Komodo dragon inhabited by The Stinger.* And then I remembered that my actual situation was worse. So between that and Jon showing up in the middle of the night, I didn't get much sleep.

We had pancakes for breakfast because my dad always makes pancakes for breakfast on Sundays. He makes them from scratch, and he uses like seventy-three bowls, so when he's done the kitchen looks like a batter bomb exploded. But they're good pancakes.

I didn't say anything during breakfast because I was tired and I was pretty sure that whatever I said would result in a lecture from my mom. Taylor didn't say anything, either, because she was listening to something on headphones. It was so loud we could all hear it.

"Turn that down!" my mom said. "You're going to ruin your ears!"

"What?" said Taylor.

"YOU'RE GOING TO RUIN YOUR EARS."

"She's ruining *my* ears," said my dad. "That doesn't sound like music. That sounds like somebody trying to kill an elephant by hitting it with electric guitars."

My dad doesn't like any music that wasn't popular when he was young. He likes bands where like half the people who were in them are dead now.

"What?" said Taylor, again.

My mom leaned over and pulled the right headphone away from Taylor's ear. "I said TURN IT DOWN."

Taylor rolled her eyes and turned it down.

"What band is that?" I asked. It didn't sound like her usual music.

"Snot House," she said.

"*What* house?" asked my dad.

"Snot."

He just shook his head, the way grown-ups do when they're thinking: *These kids today.*

"So suddenly you're a big Snot House fan, huh?" I said.

She stuck out her tongue. So far that was the highlight of my weekend.

After breakfast I went back to my room to resume being grounded. I almost fell back asleep, but then I started getting texts from Matt and Victor asking what was going on. I started to text them about Jon Aibel, but it got too complicated, so we did a three-way Skype call. When I told them about all the other animals the Bevins were bringing in, they both basically freaked out, especially when I got to the part about the ants.

"Why do they have ants?" said Matt.

"Why do they have *any* of those things?" I said.

"This Fish and Wildlife guy," said Victor. "Did he tell you what he was going to do next?"

"No," I said. "I got the feeling he thought I wouldn't be much help anyway."

"Don't you think we need to do *something*?" said Matt.

"Like what?" I said. "We tried to do something, remember? Look where it got us. We're grounded for life and Victor's drone got shot down."

"But what if those things get out? People *live* around there."

"I know, but what can *we* do about it?"

"It would help," said Victor, "if we knew what he planned to do with those things."

All three of us got quiet then, because nobody had any ideas. Before anybody came up with one, the door opened and Taylor came into my room. She was carrying a newspaper.

"Look at this," she said, shoving it in my face.

"Thanks for knocking," I said.

"What?" said Matt.

"Not you. I'm talking to Taylor."

"Just *look* at this, will you?" said Taylor.

I looked. It was a full-page ad for the Miami Zoo, which was having some kind of Halloween event.

"Taylor," I said, pushing it away. "I can't go to the zoo. I'm grounded, remember? Besides, right now I'm—"

"JUST READ IT, YOU DOPE." She shoved it back in my face.

So I read it.

Then I looked at Taylor.

"Whoa," I said.

"Yeah," she said.

"What is it?" said Victor.

"Yeah," said Matt. "What is it?"

"Do you guys have today's *Miami Herald*?" I said.

They both said they did.

"Go get the front section. Look at the back page."

"But what is it?" said Matt.

"Just go get it."

They both left, and while they were gone I read the ad again. At the top was a big color drawing of a creepy-looking pumpkin with a grinning mouth full of jagged teeth. The eyeholes were glowing circles, and next to them was a letter *Z* in red, painted in what looked like blood, so with the eyeholes it spelled ZOO. Under the pumpkin it said:

Want To Do Something REALLY
Scary This Halloween?
Come See The Miami Zoo's

KILLER KRITTERS

A Once In A Lifetime Exhibit
Of The Planet's Deadliest
Land Animals

Join Us For Our Killer

Halloween Night Bash

5 TO 11 P.M.

Music! Food! Games! Things With Fangs!

See The Killer Kritters Up Close

But Don't Get Too Close

. . . . .

Under that were color photos of animals labeled with their names. The biggest one was of a Komodo dragon, taken from ground level aiming up at its head, so it looked like Godzilla getting ready to wreck a city. The caption said it was "the largest lizard on earth, and a lethal hunter."

Under that was a picture of a snake with black, spooky-looking eyes and its mouth wide open, like it was

145

about to strike. It was labeled "Black Mamba," and the caption called it "the world's deadliest snake."

Under that was a big, ugly, hairy spider labeled "Brazilian Wandering Spider." The caption said: "It's aggressive, and it's the world's most venomous spider. Its genus name—*Phoneutria*—is the ancient Greek word for 'murderess.'"

Under that was a yellowish-brown scorpion with its tail curled up over its back. The label said it was a "Deathstalker Scorpion." Like all scorpions, it looked like some kind of gross mutant lobster, the absolute last thing you would want crawling on you. "Its sting can kill you," said the caption.

Under that was a picture of a poison dart frog, which was actually kind of cool looking. It had a bright yellow-and-black pattern on its skin, which according to the label "secretes a deadly toxin sometimes used on the tips of poison blow darts."

Near the bottom, above the information about how to see the exhibit, was a picture of an ant. It was just an ant, but in a way it was the scariest picture on the page because it had this big head with two nasty-looking pincers.

I shivered a little just looking at it, thinking about the pincers going into my skin. The label said "Siafu, or African Driver Ants." The caption said: "They may be small, but they swarm by the millions, devouring everything in their path. You don't want to get in their way."

146

"Okay," said Victor, back on Skype. He held up the zoo ad. "This is weird."

"Yeah," I said. "*Really* weird."

Now Matt was back, also holding the newspaper. "It looks like a pretty cool exhibit," he said. "But we can't go, right? I mean, we're grounded."

He can be *such* an idiot.

"Matt," I said, "we're not talking about *going* to the exhibit."

"We're not?"

"Didn't you notice what animals are *in* the exhibit?"

He looked at the pictures for a few seconds, then said, "Ohhhh."

"Yeah."

"So," said Victor, "why would Bevin be collecting the same animals as the zoo has in their exhibit?"

"Could it possibly be just a coincidence?" I said.

"That would be some coincidence," said Victor.

"We should tell Jon about this," said Taylor.

"Who's Jon?" said Victor.

"Taylor's new boyfriend," I said, leaning back to avoid the punch Taylor threw at me. "He's the Fish and Wildlife guy I was telling you about."

"We need to tell him," said Taylor, "about the zoo thing."

"I think maybe she's right," said Victor. "There has to be

some connection between Bevin and the zoo. Maybe this Jon guy will know what it is."

"Okay," I said. "I'll tell him."

"I'll see if I can find anything out," said Victor. "Maybe there's been something else in the newspaper."

"What should I do?" asked Matt.

"Just keep thinking," I said.

"Okay!" he said. Apparently he thought I was serious.

We agreed we'd let each other know if anybody found out anything new, then ended the Skype session. I took a picture of the zoo ad and texted it to Jon with a message that that said: *check out the animals*. I waited a minute for an answer, but didn't get one. Meanwhile Taylor was thumbing away on her phone.

"Okay," she said, standing up. "I'm going to Marissa's house."

I looked at her. "Wait a minute. Didn't you say Marissa lives in Bay Estates?"

She smiled. "Yup. And guess who lives right next door."

"Really? The Bevins?"

"Yup."

"Taylor, don't go over there."

"I'll be careful."

"Taylor, seriously, they're dangerous. The animals *and* the people."

"I *promise* I'll be careful," she said, opening the door.

"Yeah, but—"

She was gone.

Here's the weird thing. For as long as I could remember, if you asked me what I thought about my sister, I'd have told you she was the most annoying person on the planet. Which she definitely was. But all of a sudden, now that she was involved in . . . Well, I really didn't know what she was involved in. But I knew I was the reason she was. And now, weirdly, I was worried about my annoying sister, who was out there trying to do something about it—whatever it was—while I was stuck in my room, possibly for eternity.

I tried to think of something I could do from my room. But I couldn't think of anything except how tired I was. Pretty soon, still trying to think, I fell asleep.

Just call me Captain Action.

CHAPTER 22

I woke up to the sound of my phone burping. There were two texts right in a row. The first one was from Jon, about the zoo ad:

trying to figure this out. talk later

The second text was from Victor:

call me

I decided to check on Taylor first. She wasn't in her room,

which made me a little worried because it was getting dark. Also I felt guilty sleeping while she was trying to find stuff out. I went to the family room. My dad was on the sofa, watching the Dolphins, who were playing the Jets. Just so you know, if you're from Miami, you hate the Jets. I'm not sure *why* you do. You just do. I even hate them, and I'm not really into football.

"Dad," I said, "do you know where Tay—"

"Why do they do this to me?" he said, staring at the screen.

"Do what?" I said.

"This!" he said, pointing at the TV. "Third and eight! And they do this!"

"What did they do?"

"THEY RAN." Finally he looked at me. "Why do they DO that?"

"I don't know," I said. This was true: I honestly didn't know.

"On third and eight," he said. "Third and eight!"

"Huh. Do you know if—"

"Not third and one. Not third and two. Third and eight! THIRD. AND. EIGHT."

"Huh," I said. "Anyway, about Taylor, do—"

"YOU HAVE TO THROW THE BALL!" he said.

"Right. So do you—"

"THIS IS THE NFL! YOU HAVE TO PUT IT IN THE AIR!"

"No question," I said, leaving the family room. I found my mom in the bedroom, watching a movie on TV. She's not into sports.

"Don't go into the family room," I told her. "Dad's pretty upset about the Dolphins."

"Why?" she said.

"They didn't throw the ball."

"Huh," she said. She seemed to take it pretty well.

"Do you know where Taylor is?" I said.

"She's at Marissa's."

"Shouldn't she be home by now?"

"She'll be home soon. Marissa's mom is bringing her. She just texted me." She frowned. "Why do you want to know where Taylor is?"

"I don't!" I said. "Really, I don't. I was just . . . wondering."

She was giving me a suspicious look now because this was probably the first time in my entire life I ever acted like I cared about Taylor. "You better not be up to something."

"I'm not, seriously."

"Well you better not be. You're already in a lot of trouble."

I went back into the family room. Dad was still mad, but now it was about a new thing.

"YOU CALL THAT PUNT COVERAGE?" he said.

He looked at me. "YOU CALL THAT TACKLING?"

I didn't answer because I was pretty sure these were what Mrs. Padmore, my English teacher, would call rhetorical questions.

"MY GRANDMOTHER COULD TACKLE BETTER THAN THAT. AND SHE'S BEEN DEAD FOR SIXTEEN YEARS."

I kept on walking, back to my room. I closed the door and called Victor, who answered right away.

"Okay," he said. "This is interesting."

"What?"

"I did some Googling. It turns out Frank Bevin is the leader of a group of money guys who want to build this giant new development called MegaDade. It's like this whole new city—office buildings, houses, condos, apartments, stores, restaurants, lakes, pools, golf courses, clubs, all kinds of stuff. The biggest development in Dade County ever. Guess where they want to build it?"

"I give up."

"Right next to the zoo."

"Really?"

"Really. And guess what else?"

"What?"

"To build it, they need this big chunk of empty land that belongs to the county, which also owns the zoo. The people who run the zoo are planning to expand onto the empty land. They have all these plans for new exhibits. But now Bevin's group is trying to get the county to sell the land to them instead. So there's this big fight between Bevin's group and the zoo people over who will get the land. The county commissioners are supposed to vote on it November first, which is Tuesday."

"This Tuesday," I said. "The day after tomorrow."

"Also the day after Halloween. According to the *Miami Herald*, the zoo is probably going to win, but it's really close. If they lose a couple of votes, Bevin's group will get the land."

"Okay," I said. "This *has* to have something to do with why Bevin is collecting dangerous animals."

"Yeah," said Victor. "But what?"

"Okay," I said. "Maybe Bevin's going to show his snakes and stuff to the commissioners and say, look, the zoo has all these dangerous things, so you can't trust them."

"That doesn't make sense," said Victor. "The zoo already *has* the dangerous animals. Bevin could just point that out. He wouldn't have to go to all this trouble to bring in his own. Plus, by having them he's breaking the law. So *he'd* be the one who looked bad."

"So what's he planning to do?"

While we were thinking about that, I got another call.

"Jon's calling," I told Victor. "I'll call you later."

154

I disconnected Victor and answered Jon. "Hello?"

"Wyatt, it's Jon. That Halloween thing at the zoo, that is *weird*. That can't be coincidence. There has to be a connection. But I can't figure out what."

"Well, there's something else that might be connected."

"What?"

"Okay, Victor found out that Frank Bevin . . ."

"Who's Victor?"

"A kid I know. He lives across the canal from the Bevins. He's real smart. And he knows about what's going on."

"Okay, what did Victor find out?"

So I told him about the MegaDade project and the land that Bevin wanted to take away from the zoo, and that the commissioners were going to vote on it November first. When I was done, he was quiet for a little while. Then he said, "This is bad."

"What is?"

"I think I know what's Bevin's planning. And if I'm right, it's really bad."

"What is?" I said again.

"Can't talk now. I have to check some stuff out. I'll get back to you. This is *really* bad."

Before I could ask him a third time, he disconnected.

I was about to call Victor back when Taylor opened my door.

"Knock-knock," she said.

"You're back," I said, trying not to let her see that I was actually glad.

"You missed me!" she said.

"No, I didn't."

"Really? Then how come you asked mom where I was?" Busted.

"Never mind that," I said. "What's going on in Bay Estates?"

She came in, closed the door, and sat on my bed. "Well," she said, "at first I couldn't see anything because the Bevins have this giant wall around their whole yard."

"Yeah, I know."

"So I went over there."

"You did? How?"

"Marissa and I went over there to sell Girl Scout cookies."

"You're not a Girl Scout."

"I know. Neither is Marissa. And we didn't have any Girl Scout cookies. So Marissa got a package of Oreos from her kitchen, and we used those."

"And they actually believed you were Girl Scouts?"

"Sure. We just acted cute." She batted her eyes.

"So what happened?"

"We rang the doorbell and this guy came to the door.

Not one of the Bevins. A big guy. He said they didn't need any Girl Scout cookies. So I asked him if we could please use the bathroom. I could tell he didn't really want to let us in, but we were all 'please, mister, please please *please*.'" She batted her eyelashes again.

"Stop doing that with your eyes," I said.

"I'm just demonstrating my espionage technique," she said. "Anyway, he finally let us inside and showed us where the bathroom was. He stood right there in the hall, like keeping an eye on us. So I went into the bathroom first, and when I came out I whispered to Marissa, on her way in, to pretend she got locked in there. So she went in the bathroom, and I wandered down the hall a little and said, 'This is such a lovely home!' And the guy said, 'Please stay here.' And then Marissa pounded on the bathroom door and said, 'I can't open the door!' So the guy went to the door, and while he was doing that I scooted down the hall and around the corner into the living room. They have a *really* nice living room."

"I know," I said. "I saw it."

"So, like ten seconds later the guy came around the corner and said, 'Hey! You're not supposed to be here.' And I said, 'Oh, I'm just admiring the lovely home.' And he said, 'I'm sorry, but you have to go now.' So we left."

"So that's it? They have a nice living room? That's your espionage report?"

"No. When I was in the living room, I could see the backyard."

She waited, annoyingly, for me to ask her what she saw. I sighed. "Okay, what did you see?"

"Two trucks."

"What kind of trucks?"

"Big boxy ones. Like those big U-Haul trucks. Except they were white, and they said Gomez Party Rentals on the side. They were parked back there between these, like, hills they have in their backyard. I was gonna try to get a closer look, but the guy came and said we had to go."

"Trucks," I said.

"Yeah. And I don't think they're really for party rentals."

"I don't, either."

"I think they're to move those creepy animals."

I nodded, and looked out the window, thinking about the trucks. It was dark outside. It suddenly hit me that the next day was Monday, which meant school, and I had a ton of homework to do. It seemed stupid to be worried about homework with all this other stuff going on, but the last thing I wanted to do was get into any more trouble with my parents, especially my mom.

"We should call Jon," said Taylor. "About the trucks."

"He's doing something right now," I said.

"How do you know?"

"He called just before you got here." I told her about the MegaDade project and the zoo property. "Jon said he wanted to check something out, and he'd get back to me."

"When he gets back to you, you have to let me talk to him," she said. "So I can tell him about the trucks."

"I can tell him about the trucks."

"No! I want to tell him. I'm the one who did the espionage."

"Also he's cute."

"Very."

"Okay, you can tell him."

There was a knock on the door.

"What," I said.

My mom opened the door. "Wyatt, it's time for—" She stopped when she saw Taylor.

"You're here," she said.

"Yes," said Taylor.

"In Wyatt's room."

"Yes."

My mom looked at me. "Taylor's in your room."

"Yes.

"And you're fine with that."

"Yes."

She stared at us. "What's going on? WHAT ARE YOU TWO UP TO?"

"We were just talking," said Taylor.

"Just talking," said my mom. "Right. You two, who *never* have a polite conversation, who get along the way North Korea gets along with South Korea, who can't decide on what pizza toppings to get without starting a nuclear war, you were just sitting around having a cordial conversation."

Taylor and I nodded.

Mom stared at us for a few more seconds, then said, "Are you kids doing drugs?"

"What? No!" I said.

"Mom!" said Taylor.

"Well," said my mom, "whatever is going on here, I don't like it, you hear me?"

"You don't like us having a cordial conversation?" said Taylor.

"Don't you get smart with *me*, young lady. You two wash up. Dinner's ready. Your father will not be joining us. He's in mourning."

We washed up and went to the kitchen, passing my dad, who was lying on the sofa, staring at the ceiling. The TV was off.

"They lost?" I said.

He looked at me and said, "A screen pass. In that situation. A SCREEN PASS."

"Unbelievable," I said. It seemed like the right thing.

He looked back at the ceiling. We left him that way.

For dinner we had my mom's *arroz con pollo*, which is a Cuban dish, chicken and rice, that's really good. Taylor and I were careful not to say anything nice to each other. After dinner I told my mom I had homework, and went to my room. I opened my trigonometry book and read for maybe eleven seconds before I fell asleep. That's the kind of scholar I am.

Somewhere in the middle of my ninety-third weird dream, I woke up. I looked at my phone. It was 1:14 a.m.

Then I realized what woke me up.

Tap-tap-tap-tap.

I jumped out of bed and looked out. Jon was making an open-the-window motion.

I opened it and he climbed in.

"This is bad," he said. "This is *really* bad."

CHAPTER 23

"**W**hat is it?" I said.

"I went down to the zoo," he said, "to check out the—"

He stopped, because Taylor had opened the door. Either she was the world's lightest sleeper, or she'd been staying up in case Jon appeared.

"Hi, Jon," she said, closing the door behind her.

"Sure, come on in," I said.

"Hi, Taylor," said Jon.

"What's that smell?" I said.

"Nothing," she said.

162

"It's perfume! It's the middle of the night and you put on *perfume*." It smelled like at least a gallon.

"Shut up," said Taylor. She turned to Jon. "They have trucks."

"Who does?" he said.

"The Bevins. I did some espionage." She told him about the trucks.

"Taylor," he said, "that was very dangerous, going over there."

"I know!" she said. If you guessed that she also batted her eyelashes, you're getting to know my sister.

"But you're confirming what I suspected," said Jon. "The trucks . . . It makes sense."

Taylor stuck her tongue out at me.

"What makes sense?" I said.

"Okay, let me back up," said Jon. "Like I was saying, I went down to the zoo to check out the Halloween exhibit. It's at the far end from the main entrance, which means it's near the fence separating the zoo from the open land that Bevin wants to buy. It's pretty overgrown back there—I walked around—but there's a dirt road that runs near the fence, right behind the building where they have the Killer Kritters."

"So trucks could get in there," said Taylor.

"Yup."

"Okay," I said, "but why would Bevin take his animals

to the zoo, which already has the exact same animals? That doesn't make any sense."

"I'm afraid it does," said Jon. "Although I'm still having trouble believing it."

"Believing what?"

"Here's what I think is going to happen. Tomorrow night is the big Halloween party at the Killer Kritters exhibit. Actually, it's already tomorrow, so the party's tonight. Anyway, I asked around down at the zoo; they're expecting a lot of people. At some point during that party, after it gets dark, the two trucks are going to drive up the dirt road on the other side of the fence. They're going to be carrying the crates with Bevin's collection. They're going to open the crates, and they're going to release the animals."

"Seriously?" I said. "They're just going to *let them go*?"

"I think that's what's going to happen."

"Right next to the zoo fence."

"Yes. With a couple thousand people milling around on the other side, just a few feet away."

"But the fence would keep the people safe," said Taylor.

Jon shook his head. "No," he said. "I had a good look at that fence. It's industrial chain link, ten feet high with barbed wire on top. It's great for keeping people out. But it's not going to stop a snake from getting in, or a spider, or a scorpion. It's definitely not going to stop ants."

164

"What about a Komodo dragon?" I said.

"It'd have a little more trouble, but I think that bad boy could work his way under the fence."

"But why would Bevin do that?" I said. "I mean, those animals, with all those people around . . . Why?"

"Money," said Jon. "A *lot* of money. I did some research, following up on what your friend Victor found out. It turns out that Frank Bevin's financial empire is shaky. *Very* shaky, according to rumors. He's had some major deals go bad, and he owes a lot of money. So basically he's betting everything on this MegaDade project. He really needs it to succeed, which means he really needs the county to sell him the land next to the zoo. He and his people have been leaning hard on the county commissioners, but right now they don't have enough votes. The zoo's very popular, and most of the commissioners think they'll look bad if they vote against the zoo to help some rich guy.

"So lately—this is what caught my attention—Bevin's people have been claiming that the zoo is badly managed, and might even be a hazard to the community. They specifically mentioned the Killer Kritters exhibit. They claimed it was a safety risk. The zoo people were angry about that, said they were very careful and the exhibit is totally safe, which is true. And so far everybody believes the zoo. But imagine what will happen if tomorrow night, at the big Halloween party, a black mamba or a deathstalker scorpion gets loose in that crowd."

"But wouldn't they know it's not from the zoo?" I said. "I mean, all the zoo animals would still be in their cages."

"Right, and that's exactly what the zoo people would say. But nobody would believe them. Everybody would think that somehow some animals got out. I mean, if the zoo has an exhibit of Brazilian wandering spiders, and a visitor gets bit by a Brazilian wandering spider, nobody's going to think it didn't come from the zoo. The zoo is going to look really bad."

"But if that spider bites somebody . . ." said Taylor. "Or that mamba snake . . ."

"Yeah," said Jon. "Somebody could be seriously hurt. Or worse. *Much* worse. When the driver ants come out, after being cooped up in there . . . You would *not* want to be in their way."

"And you really believe Bevin would do that?" I said. "For a land deal?"

"He's a desperate man. And it's a *lot* of money."

"Wow," I said. "This is bad."

"Yup," said Jon.

"We can't let this happen," said Taylor. "We have to tell the police, right?"

"I did," said Jon.

"What?" I said. "When?"

"Before I came here. I went in and tried to tell them what was going on. But the second I mentioned the name Bevin, they told me to hold on, that they had to contact my bosses. Then they told me some Fish and Wildlife guys were coming over to hear what I had to say. Remember when I told you I had a police source?"

"Yes."

"While I'm sitting there in the waiting room, I get a text from him. Tells me my bosses told the cops I'm mentally unstable and they're sending somebody over to take me in for psychological evaluation."

"Meaning what?"

"Meaning, basically, arrest me. Like I told you, Bevin has very powerful friends, and whoever they are, they're leaning hard on my bosses to get me out of the way."

"So what'd you do?" said Taylor.

"I ran away. Said I had to use the bathroom, climbed out the window, and took off. So now I'm a lunatic *and* a fugitive. I can't even go back to my apartment."

"Wow," said Taylor.

"Yeah," said Jon.

"So now what?" I said.

"Now I have to try to stop Bevin without any help from the police. In fact, I have to try to stop Bevin while *avoiding* the police, not to mention Fish and Wildlife."

"How're you going to do that?"

He shook his head. "I have no idea."

"We'll help you," said Taylor.

"No. Absolutely not. I don't want either of you to go anywhere near the Bevins, or the zoo. It's way, way too dangerous. I only came here because I wanted somebody besides me to know what was going on, in case . . . Just in case. But it's my problem. You two have to stay out of it." He looked at Taylor, then me. "You understand?"

We nodded.

Jon looked at his phone. "Okay, it's late. I need to find somewhere to catch some sleep."

"You can stay here!" said Taylor.

"Thanks, but no. I'll find a park or something, get a little sleep. I still have more than twelve hours until the zoo thing. I'll figure something out." He tried to smile, but it wasn't much of a smile.

"You guys go to sleep," he said. "Tomorrow's a school day."

He opened the window and climbed out. He looked back and said, "Thanks for your help, guys. Really." Then he closed the window and was gone.

Taylor looked at me. "How's he going to stop them, all by himself?"

"I don't know."

"Wyatt, we *have* to help him."

"How?"

She stared at the window. "I don't know."

"Me, either. And I have to be at school in five hours. So right now I'm going to take his advice and try to get some sleep. You should, too."

"Yeah," she said. "I guess so."

She opened the door and went into the hall. "Happy Halloween," she said. She closed the door.

"Yeah," I said, to nobody. "Happy Halloween."

CHAPTER

24

You know what's weird?

What's weird is getting on a bus and going to school on a Monday morning after you spent the weekend getting accused of stealing and being threatened with jail by the police, then getting visited twice in the middle of the night by a fugitive federal agent who tells you that a supposedly respectable businessman is planning to let some of the world's deadliest animals loose in a crowd of innocent people.

That's what's weird.

All around me on the bus, kids were talking about their

weekends, soccer games, homework, Halloween plans—
normal human stuff like that. I didn't talk to anybody until
Matt and Victor got on the bus. I told them what Jon thought
Bevin was planning to do at the zoo party. It took a while for
them to understand what I was saying, and when they did,
they freaked out, especially Matt, who said, way too loud,
"HE'S GOING TO LET THE MAMBO SNAKE GO?"
Which caused everybody to look at us.

"Quiet," I said. "And it's mam*ba* snake."

"I thought it was mambo."

"That's a dance, you moron."

"We have to tell the police," said Victor.

"Jon tried that." I said. "They tried to arrest him. He's
hiding."

"So what's he going to do?"

"He said he'd try to figure something out."

"That doesn't sound like much of a plan."

"No."

"Maybe we can do something."

"Like what?"

"What if we can stop the trucks?"

"How would we do that?"

"I don't know yet. But if the trucks can't leave the Bevin
house, the animals can't get to the zoo. Maybe we could do
something to them."

"Okay," I said, "except number one, I'm grounded. I have to go straight home after school."

"Me too," said Matt.

"Number two, there's guys over at the Bevin house. And the trucks are in the backyard. They won't let you just walk in and mess with them."

Victor looked out the window. "I'll keep thinking," he said.

I nodded. I was glad *somebody* was thinking. I was too tired to do it myself.

When the bus got to school we got off and trudged into the courtyard, heading for the clot of kids we usually hung out with in the morning. Thirty seconds after we got there, Suzana showed up. I figured she'd ignore me, but she walked right over to me.

"Is it true?" she said.

"Is what true?"

"That you went over to Troy and Nick's house and stole Nick's Apple watch?"

"No!"

"Then how come I saw you in a video climbing over their wall and going into their house?"

"You saw the video?"

"Troy sent it to me."

Of course he did.

"Okay," I said. "I did go to their house. But I didn't steal that watch."

"You mean the watch that the police found in your bedroom?"

"I didn't put it there!"

"Then how did it get there?"

"They put it there! To set me up!"

By now I was shouting, and kids were staring. Suzana was looking at me like I was crazy, which I guess is how I sounded. I tried to make myself calm down. "Listen, Suzana," I said. "You know me. I'm not crazy. And I'm not a thief. You're my friend. You *know* me."

"I thought I did. But I also saw the video of you in the Bevins' house. Wyatt, this whole thing you have about Nick and Troy . . . To be honest, you've been acting crazy. I know them. They're nice guys."

"No they're not, Suzana. And you *don't* know them. They're nice to *you*. But they're not nice guys, and their dad is a really bad guy. I found some stuff out about him this weekend, and it's scary. If you just—"

"What's scary?" said Troy, suddenly appearing between me and Suzana.

"Yeah," said Nick, coming up behind Troy. "What's scary?"

"Nothing," I said.

"No, really," said Troy. "Tell us about the scary thing."

All three of them were looking at me, waiting. I could see pity in Suzana's eyes. She was feeling sorry for me, her former friend turned crazy person.

"Never mind," I said. I turned around and walked over to where Matt and Victor were standing. Pretty much everybody was watching me. My face felt like it was on fire.

"So, Suzana," said Troy, loud enough for me to hear. "You coming to the Grove tonight?"

The Grove is Coconut Grove. There's a massive street party there every Halloween.

"Absolutely," said Suzana.

"Okay, we'll meet you there," said Troy. "Say eight o'clock, in front of CocoWalk?"

"Sounds good," said Suzana.

"See you then," said Troy.

As they left, they walked past me. "Hey, Nick," said Troy. "What time is it?"

"Let me check my expensive Apple watch." He looked at me. "No, better wait till there's no thieves around."

They walked away, smiling big Hollister-face smiles.

I looked at Suzana, thinking maybe I could try to convince her that I wasn't crazy. She had her back turned to me. She was talking with her hot popular girlfriends.

The bell rang. Everybody started walking to class. I was so

weirded out, it took me a few seconds to remember that my first class that day was Human Geography, which sounds like it should be about body parts but is actually not. It's about stuff humans do on the earth. For example, they form cities, which in Human Geography is called urbanization. That's what we were studying, and we were supposed to have written five paragraphs about it for homework. Unfortunately for me, I had written zero paragraphs, so the teacher, who, unfortunately for him, is named Mr. Gurk, gave me a zero.

So my day was off to a great start.

Nothing terrible happened in my next couple of classes. Then I had English, which meant I was going to see Suzana again. Mrs. Padmore was sick that day, so we had a substitute teacher. I feel kind of sorry for substitutes because they usually don't know what's going on, and kids sometimes take advantage of them. Like, one time, in Trigonometry, we had this substitute who was pretty clueless, even for a substitute. A couple of kids actually managed to convince her that we were studying subtraction. She was like, "Really? You're studying subtraction in ninth grade?" And the kids were like, "Yes! We're the mathematically disabled class. They didn't tell you?" So she spent the whole period putting subtraction problems on the board, and we pretended to have a hard time solving them. It was kind of mean, I guess. But it got us a vacation from the hypotenuse.

Anyway, the substitute in English class was the kind of sub—every student's favorite kind—who just wants to be left alone. We were supposedly studying *Romeo and Juliet*, and he told us to read Act III quietly to ourselves. Then he propped his head in his hands and, as far as we could tell, went to sleep. Kids started talking, texting, playing games on their phones, doing pretty much anything except reading Act III of *Romeo and Juliet*. I tried to think about the Bevin situation, but I was really tired. I put my head down on my desk to see if that would help me think.

"Hey."

I jerked my head up. Suzana was poking my arm. She had switched seats and was now sitting next to me.

"Wake up," she said.

"I wasn't sleeping," I said. "I was thinking."

"Well you snore when you think."

"Good to know. Is that why you woke me up?"

"No. I want to talk to you."

"About how suddenly I'm crazy?"

"Basically, yes. It bothers me, Wyatt. I mean, we're friends. Or I thought we were. We've been through stuff."

"I know. That's why I figured you'd at least listen to me."

She nodded. "Okay, I'm listening."

"Really?"

"Really."

"Promise you won't interrupt until I'm done? Even if it seems weird?"

"I promise I won't interrupt. I can't promise I'll believe you."

So I told her everything, starting with me and Matt sneaking into the Bevins' house to get Frank back, and ending with Jon's second visit to my house that morning. She didn't interrupt, but she frowned a lot, especially when I told her about Jon and what he thought the Bevins were planning to do.

When I was done, she was quiet for a few seconds, then said, "And this Jon guy . . . You believe him?"

"Yeah."

"You believe he's really a federal wildlife agent? Running around tapping on bedroom windows in the middle of the night?"

"I do."

"Do you have any proof that he's who he says he is? Did he show you any official ID or anything?"

"No, but—"

"Was he at least wearing a uniform?"

"No." It didn't seem like a good time to bring up the Snot House shirt.

"You realize how this sounds, right?" she said.

"How does it sound?"

"It sounds like you're crazy. It sound like you made up this imaginary guy to excuse stealing the watch. Or, if you didn't make him up, it sounds like *he's* crazy. Or you're *both* crazy."

"Great. Thanks, friend."

"Seriously, Wyatt. Think about it. You're asking me to believe that the Bevins, a successful and well-known family in the community, are planning to do this horrible thing that could get innocent people killed. AND you're asking me to believe that this federal agent knows about it, and he even told the police, and nobody's doing anything."

"That's right."

"You don't think that sounds crazy? Seriously, tell me."

What I wanted to say was, "Okay, fine, don't believe me. Tomorrow, after there's been a horrible tragedy at the zoo, I can say I told you so." And I almost did say that. But then I had another idea.

"Okay," I said. "If I'm crazy, then there's nothing danger-ous about the zoo party tonight, right?"

"Right."

"So why don't you go?"

"What?"

"You're supposed to meet your new boyfriends Nick and Troy in the Grove tonight, right?"

"They're not my boyfriends. But yes, we're meeting in the Grove."

"Okay, so instead of the Grove, tell them you want to go to the party at the zoo."

"Why would I do that?"

"To prove I'm crazy. Tell them you're a big fan of the zoo, and you really want to go and see the Killer Kritters. Say you don't have a ride. Beg them to take you. Bat your eyelashes. You know how to do it. See what they say. If they say okay, they'll take you, then I'm crazy. But if they won't take you, or they say you shouldn't go, then you have to ask yourself, why not? What are they afraid of? What do they know?"

"That's ridiculous."

"Okay, then. Don't ask them. Go to the Grove tonight; have fun. Forget about your crazy ex-friend Wyatt and his imaginary Fish and Wildlife agent. But watch the news tomorrow morning. Just to make sure I'm really crazy."

She shook her head. "I don't need to make sure." She stood up. "I'm sorry, Wyatt. You need help."

She went back to her desk. I put my head back down on mine.

CHAPTER 25

"**O**kay," said Victor. "I think I have an idea for stopping the trucks."

Victor, Matt, and I were back on the bus, heading home. All around us kids were talking about their Halloween plans. In Miami, high-school kids usually don't go trick-or-treating. They roam around in groups, mostly just hanging out but sometimes doing stuff like throwing eggs at people's houses, which is a Halloween tradition that I think was started by the druids.

"I have an idea, too," said Matt. "Potatoes."

"Potatoes?" I said. "To stop the trucks?"

"Yeah," said Matt. "I saw it on the Internet. You stick a potato in the whaddycallit—tailpipe. Then the motor stops."

"Are you serious?" I said. "A potato?"

"Actually," said Victor, "that does work sometimes."

"It does?" I'm always surprised when Matt is right about something.

"Yeah," Victor said. "I actually thought about doing it that way. The problem is, you need to really jam the potato into the pipe, or the exhaust pressure blows it right back out when the engine starts. We can't do that because we can't get to the trucks when they're parked in the backyard. We're going to have to get them when they're moving."

"So what's your idea?"

"Road stars."

"What's a road star?"

"It's a metal thing, with spikes, and the way it's designed there's always a spike pointing up. You put it on the road, and when a tire rolls over it, it gets punctured. They're mainly for police or the military, but sometimes people use them to stop people from driving on their lawns."

"Great," I said. "But where do you get road stars?"

"I Googled it, and there's this chain store called the Spy Cellar. They sell surveillance cameras and stuff like that, but they also have road stars. There's a store in South Miami."

"I've seen that store," I said. "In a strip mall on Dixie Highway."

"Yeah. I'll ride my bike over there when I get home. It's nineteen ninety-five for a pack of four. I'll get a couple of packs."

"Cool," said Matt. "Road stars."

"Wait," I said. "How is this gonna work? We just stand out in front of the Bevin house, holding road stars, waiting for the trucks? Won't we be kind of obvious?"

"Not tonight," said Victor. "That's the good part. It's Halloween. There will be kids in the streets all over Bay Estates. We just put on costumes and blend in. We hang around until the trucks come out. Then one of us wanders into the street, so they have to stop. The other two put road stars under the tires. Then the one in front gets out of the way and the trucks roll over the road stars. The whole thing should only take a few seconds."

Victor had really thought it out. Suddenly this seemed like a real thing that might actually happen: us against the trucks.

Then I remembered something.

"Wait a minute," I said. "I'm grounded."

"Oh man, that's right," said Matt. "My parents won't let me out tonight. *Especially* not tonight."

Victor looked at me, then Matt, then back at me. "Okay," he said. "I guess I'll have to try to do it alone."

I tried to picture that.

"No," I said. "We'll be there."

"We will?" said Matt. "How?"

"I don't know," I said. "But we will."

CHAPTER

26

I stared out my bedroom window, waiting for the sun to finish setting. It was taking forever.

Outside, Halloween had already started. We'd had a couple of early trick-or-treaters, little kids in *Frozen* princess dresses and Buzz Lightyear costumes who went around the neighborhood with their parents following close behind. Every time the doorbell rang, Csonka would go charging to the front door, barking like a maniac to let us know that the doorbell had rung, which Csonka considered to be the most exciting thing that ever happened in the history of the universe, no matter how many times it happened. To add to the noise level, every now and then a firecracker went off in the distance. Basically every holiday in Miami, including Christmas, involves setting off firecrackers. New Year's Eve sounds like World War III.

I'd spent the afternoon worrying and texting. I texted Jon four times, telling him what we were planning to do and asking him what was going on. He finally answered me, with three words: *busy talk later.* I exchanged a bunch of texts with Victor. He told me he went to the Spy Cellar, and the sales guy there wasn't too happy about selling road stars to a kid, especially on Halloween. But Victor finally talked the guy into selling him one package. So he had four road stars. He told me he figured the trucks would leave the Bevin backyard sometime after dark, so he planned to be outside the Bevin house, wearing a Darth Vader costume, at sunset, which according to him was going to be at seven twenty-eight p.m.

I told him I'd be there. But the truth was, I still didn't know how I was going to escape from my house. Matt had texted me that his plan was to just sneak out his window. That actually made sense because Matt's parents are as clueless as he is. There was a good chance they'd never even notice he was gone. My parents were not that clueless. My dad had cut a piece of wood and wedged it in my window frame from the outside so I couldn't open it from the inside.

"I'm sorry, Wyatt," my mom said. "I wish we didn't have

to do this. But right now we don't feel like we can trust you."

The thing is, they were right. They *couldn't* trust me. I was definitely planning to sneak out. I had a good reason to do it, but they'd never believe me. If I told them that I needed to go throw road stars under a truck full of deadly animals headed for the zoo, they'd make me go see a psychiatrist.

But I really did have to go. The question was how. That's what I was worrying about as Halloween day was turning into Halloween night. I had pretty much made up my mind that my only option was to just go out the front door and take off. I'd have to accept whatever punishment I got when I came back home. Death, probably. But I couldn't think of any other way.

Then Taylor knocked on my door and, without waiting for me to invite her, came into my room, closed the door, and sat down on my bed.

"So," she said. "What's your plan?"

"What makes you think I have a plan?"

She rolled her eyes. "Wyatt, please. I'm not an idiot. What's your plan?"

So I told her about Victor and the road stars. She nodded.

"I like it," she said.

"One problem," I said, pointing to my window. "I can't get out."

She looked at the window and nodded again.

"Wait here," she said, and left the room.

Sometimes my sister scares me.

I texted Jon again. I didn't really expect an answer, and I didn't get one. I stared out the window, listening to the sounds of Halloween.

Ten minutes went by, and Taylor was back. This time she didn't even bother to knock. She just came in and sat down on my bed.

"Okay," she said. "I can get you out of the house without Mom and Dad knowing."

"How?"

"Before I tell you, you have to promise something."

"What?"

"I'm going with you."

"Taylor, no. It's too dangerous."

"Okay, then you can stay here. I'll go to Bay Estates. I'm not the one who's grounded with my window blocked shut." She got up.

I sighed. "Okay," I said. "What's your plan?"

"First, promise me I can go."

"I promise you can go."

She sat back down. "Second thing, do you have twenty dollars?"

"I think so."

"Give it to me."

"Why?"

"To pay Dylan."

"Dylan Schweitzer?" This was a kid in my sister's grade who lived two doors from us.

"Yes."

"Why am I paying him twenty dollars?"

"He has a horse costume."

"I'm paying him twenty dollars for a horse costume?"

"That's part of it."

"I don't understand."

So she explained her plan.

Like I said, sometimes my sister scares me.

CHAPTER 27

It worked exactly the way Taylor said it would.

At seven p.m. sharp, Dylan Schweitzer appeared at our house, carrying the horse costume. It was a two-person costume. One person got into the front part of the horse, occupying the horse's head and front legs. The other person got into the back part, becoming the horse's back legs and butt. The two parts of the costume attached together in the middle by Velcro strips. Taylor announced to my parents that she and Dylan were going to go trick-or-treating together as a horse. This probably struck them as a little bit strange, since

Taylor and Dylan weren't close friends. But they liked Dylan, and Taylor was always doing strange things.

Taylor, Dylan, and my parents stood around chatting for a minute or two. Then some trick-or-treaters rang the doorbell, which caused Csonka to erupt. While my parents were dealing with that, Taylor and Dylan drifted back to the bedroom hallway. A minute later the trick-or-treaters were gone, and the horse came shuffling into the living room, with the back legs stumbling a little.

"Okay!" said Taylor, from inside the horse's head. "Dylan and I are going now!"

"Okay," said my mom. "Make sure you're back by ten."

"Okay," said Taylor, sticking her arm out of a hole in the horse costume and opening the door. "Bye!"

"Bye, Taylor!" said my mom to the front of the horse. "Bye, Dylan!"

"Bye!" said a muffled voice from the rear end of the horse as it stumbled out the door.

Of course that voice wasn't Dylan's. It was mine. Dylan was now in my bedroom with my twenty dollars, which he needed because his parents were making him pay for a new iPhone after he dropped his old one—for the second time—into the toilet. The plan was for him to stay in my room with the lights out, lying on my bed watching movies on Taylor's iPad, until I got back. If my parents knocked on the door, he was supposed to say, in a muffled voice, "Please leave me alone." If they opened the door, he'd pull the covers up over his head and mumble about how he just wanted to be left alone, acting sulky and pouty and miserable, exactly like a kid who was grounded on Halloween.

I had to admit, it was a pretty great plan.

What was definitely not great was being the rear end of the horse. For one thing, you have to walk bent over. For another thing, you can't see anything, so you stumble a lot. Also, you're hot and sweaty, and you're getting whiffs of the BO of all the previous people who have been in the horse, which in the case of this costume must have been the entire Miami Dolphins offensive line. After maybe a minute of walking, I was dying back there, so I undid the Velcro and stood up. This meant now Taylor and I were a two-part horse. She was the head, with just the two legs, and I was the horse's rear end, with the tail sticking out behind and my upper body sticking out the top, holding the rest of the horse up around my waist with one hand. We looked pretty stupid, but at least I could breathe.

We headed for Bay Estates, passing groups of trick-or-treaters on the way. It was getting pretty dark, and the older kids were out. We went as fast as we could, but by the time we got to the Bay Estates entrance it was past seven thirty. There were two police cars parked out front, with two officers leaning against them, watching people come and go, keeping an eye out for Halloween troublemakers. We walked past them toward the security gate. Usually to get past the security guard you have to be on a guest list, but since it was Halloween he was letting trick-or-treaters in. Taylor and I trotted past the guardhouse, a two-part horse with the butt running in front. The guard gave us a funny look but didn't stop us.

It took us five more minutes to get to the Bevin property. The house was dark. There was a black iron fence running along the entire front of the property. At the far end was a closed electric gate leading to the driveway. In the middle of the fence was a smaller gate, also closed, leading to the front walkway. As we arrived, some trick-or-treaters tried to open the gate, but it was locked. Apparently the Bevin household wasn't giving out treats tonight. The trick-or-treaters moved on down the street, toward the next Bay Estates mansion.

The street was quiet now, and the sky was totally black. I looked around, wondering if Taylor and I had gotten there too late. Then I saw Darth Vader, almost invisible in the shadows, standing under a tree at the far end of the Bevins' lot. I trotted over to him, with Taylor behind.

"Hey," I said. "Is that you?"

"Yes," said Victor's voice from inside the Darth mask. "And you're, what, a horse's butt?"

"It got me out of the house."

"Who's in the horse head? Is that Matt?"

"No, my sister."

Taylor waved her hand through the hole in the horse.

Victor nodded his mask. "The trucks are still back there. When it was light I could see them. They'll have to come out on this side of the house, where there's room next to the wall."

"You have the road stars?"

He held up a black trick-or-treat bag with a pumpkin on it. "In here. Do you know if Matt got out?"

"No."

"What's *that*?" said Taylor, pointing.

We turned and saw a shape trotting along the street toward us. It had a cone-shaped head and cone-shaped arms. When it got closer we could see that the head and arms were actually orange traffic cones. Two big round white cardboard eyes had been glued to the front of the head cone, which was held in place by a string around the neck of—you probably already guessed this—Matt. In addition to three cones, he was wearing a pair of pink rain boots.

"Did I miss it?" he said.

"What . . ." I pointed toward Matt's cone head and cone arms. "What *are* you?"

"You can't tell?"

"No." I shook my head. So did Darth Vader and the horse.

"I'm Patrick!" he said. "The starfish! From *SpongeBob*!"

Matt is a huge fan of *SpongeBob SquarePants*.

"Seriously?" I said. "You're wearing traffic cones?"

"At least I'm not a horse's rear."

He had me there.

"Who's the horse head?" said Matt.

"Me, Taylor." The horse waved its hand.

"Okay," said Victor. "Here's the plan."

We gathered around him, our dark-helmeted leader.

"They have to come out from there," he said, pointing along the right side of the Bevin house toward the backyard. "When they get to the street they'll turn right. We need to stop them early, before they get up too much speed."

"Stop them how?" said Taylor.

"I'll stand in front of them."

"What if they don't see you in that costume?"

"They'll see me." Victor pulled a lightsaber from his belt and flicked it on. It was bright red. He flicked it off. "They'll have to stop. They won't like it. They'll honk their horn. They might even get out of the truck. So you guys need to move fast."

He dug into his trick-or-treat bag and handed two road stars to me and two to Matt. They were heavier than I thought they'd be. They were made from two pieces of round

194

metal rod, bent and welded together so four ends stuck out in different directions. The ends had been sawed off at an angle to make sharp points. They looked serious.

"Wow," said Matt, hefting the two stars in his hands.

"When the trucks stop," said Victor, "go to the back truck first. Wyatt, take the right side, and Matt you take the left. Stick one of your road stars under the rear tire on your side. Then walk forward to the front truck. Walk calmly, like you're just two regular trick-or-treaters, because the guys in the back truck will be able to see you then. When you get to the front of the first truck, casually lean over and put the second star under the front tire. I'm hoping the guys in the front truck will be paying attention to me and won't notice what you're doing."

The Darth mask turned toward Matt, then me. "You guys got that?"

"I think so," said Matt.

"Back truck first," I said. "We put one star under the rear tire. Then we walk forward . . ."

"Calmly," said Victor.

"Right, walk calmly forward and casually put the second star under the front tire of the front truck. Got it."

"Then keep walking," said Victor. "Calmly. When I see you're done I'll get out of the way and the trucks will move.

Then the tires will blow. Then we all stop being calm, and run. They'll have one spare tire for each truck, so they can fix one tire. But they can't fix two. They'll be stuck here."

"Sounds good," I said, trying to sound like I believed myself.

"What do I do?" said Taylor.

"You stand by," said Victor.

"Stand by?" said Taylor. "What does that even *mean*?"

"It means be ready," said Victor. "In case."

"In case what?"

"In case we need you."

"*Hmph,*" said Taylor, making it clear, even inside the horse head, that she was not happy with standing by.

So then we waited. I sent a text to Jon telling him what our plan was. I didn't expect him to answer, but he did, right away:

trucks still there?

I texted back **yes**. He didn't answer that.

"What time is it?" said Victor.

I checked my phone. "eight fourteen." We all looked down the side of the Bevin house. It was still dark.

"They have to move soon," said Victor.

We stood around waiting some more, staring toward the

back yard. Groups of trick-or-treaters drifted by, tried the gate, moved on. Victor went over the plan one more time, but I had trouble focusing. The road stars felt heavy in my hands. I was sweating, even though it wasn't that warm. I could feel my heart pounding, and there was a hole where my stomach was supposed to be.

We waited some more. There were no trick-or-treaters for a while. It seemed very quiet.

"I have to pee," said Matt.

"Seriously?" I said. "Now?"

"Yes. Bad."

"Then pee," I said. "But hurry."

"Where?"

I waved at the darkness. "Out there. Just hurry."

He shuffled away in his traffic cones and pink rain boots, disappearing in the shadows of some trees on the other side of the street.

For a few seconds, it was quiet again.

Then Taylor grabbed my arm and said, "Look." She pointed toward the electric driveway gate.

It was opening.

In the backyard, headlight beams came on.

The trucks were coming.

CHAPTER 28

It did not go exactly the way Victor planned it.

The first problem was that Matt was across the street peeing, and he still had his two road stars.

"Matt!" I yelled. "They're coming!"

"Just a minute!" he yelled back, from the darkness. "I'm still peeing!"

"I'll get his road stars!" said Taylor, galloping off in Matt's direction.

"No time!" said Victor, moving to the right and toward the middle of the street. "Wyatt, get ready."

So apparently we were doing this with just the two of us.

I gripped my road stars, one in each hand, and stood on the side of the street. The trucks, close together, came out from alongside the house and onto the driveway. Like Taylor said, they were white and had GOMEZ PARTY RENTAL on the side. I couldn't see who was in either truck.

The trucks went through the gate, reached the street, and turned right. Victor was now standing in the middle of the street. He had turned his lightsaber on. I gripped the road stars. The trucks went past me, picking up speed. Then the driver of the first truck saw Victor and jammed on the brakes, honking. The second truck almost hit the first truck before it stopped, right in front of me.

I ran to the back tire, leaned over and put the road star down. So far, so good. Then I stood up and started walking forward along the right side of the trucks, remembering what Victor said. *Walk calmly.*

The front truck driver was blasting his horn. He rolled down his window and yelled "MOVE!" I could see Victor in the headlights, waving his lightsaber around like the truck was Luke Skywalker. Victor had guts.

Walk calmly.

I was alongside the front truck, next to the cab. The windows were open, and two people in the truck were yelling now. I didn't look as I went past them. I leaned over, as casually as I could, to put the road star under the truck's front right tire.

"HEY!"

The right-side truck door banged open, and before I could stand back up, a guy was on me. He was a big guy, wearing a white hazmat suit, like what people wear when they clean up chemical spills.

"What are you doing?" he said. I tried to run, but he grabbed my arm, tight. He was really strong, and it really hurt. He yanked me back toward him, looked down, and saw the road star gleaming in the headlights from the truck behind us.

"DON'T MOVE!" he yelled to the driver, who was still honking at Victor. Gripping my arm painfully hard, he reached down, picked up the road star, and showed it to the driver, who said a bad word. Before he could say any more, there was movement on the other side of the street. It was the horsehead, occupied by Taylor, galloping toward the front truck, a road star in each hand. Stumbling along behind her, attempting to zip up his fly despite having traffic cones on his hands, was starfish Matt. What I'm saying is, it was not a stealthy attack.

The truck driver, who was also wearing a hazmat suit, opened his door, jumped out, and yelled at them to stop. Matt did stop, but Taylor kept coming, although it wasn't clear what she thought she was going to accomplish. When she got within range, the truck driver, also a large person, took a swing at her and nailed her right in the nose. Fortunately it was the horse's nose, which was a foot or so higher than Taylor's actual nose. But he did knock her backward, sending her sprawling onto the road, and sending the two road stars she'd been holding clattering across the street into the grass.

The driver leaned over and looked like he was going to grab Taylor, but Victor—did I mention that Victor has guts?—came running around from the front of the truck, yelling something I couldn't understand, and started whacking the driver with his lightsaber.

The driver probably could have killed Victor, but I guess he decided it was time to stop fooling around with costumed kids and get out of there. He shoved Victor aside, got back into the truck, and told the guy on my side, who was still holding my arm, to get in. The guy shoved me away, jumped into the truck, and slammed the door. The driver stomped on the gas and the truck lurched forward. The second truck did the same thing. But when it moved, there was a loud *bang* from the back. That was the right rear tire blowing when it rolled over the road star I'd put there.

The first truck was accelerating away now, and the second one started to follow, but when the driver realized his tire was blown, he hit the brakes and stopped. He started honking his horn, flashing his lights, and yelling at the front truck, which also stopped. The front truck backed up, fast. Doors on both trucks opened.

Victor, Taylor, Matt, and I were watching all this from the middle of the street, a dozen or so yards behind the trucks. Victor was the first one to react.

"Come on," he said. He started running toward the trees on the property across from the Bevin house. The rest of us followed. When we reached the trees, we were all breathing pretty hard. Taylor took off her horse head and Victor took off his Vader mask. I stepped out of my horse butt. Underneath I had on shorts and sneakers. We stood in the shadows and watched what was happening back on the street.

The trucks had stopped near a streetlight, so we could see them pretty well. There were four guys, two from each truck, all four wearing hazmat suits. They had flashlights and were at the back of the second truck, looking at the blown tire. They said some bad words and some other stuff I couldn't hear much of, except it was pretty clear they thought we were just random Halloween kids being vandals. That was good. At least they didn't know we knew what was in the trucks. They huddled together and talked for a minute or so. Then they went to the back of the truck. They looked around to see if anybody was there, then raised the cargo door.

A flashlight beam lit up the inside. Practically the first

thing it hit was the head of the Komodo dragon, pressed against the side of a big wire cage.

"Holy crap," said Taylor. "You weren't kidding."

"No," I said.

One of the men climbed up into the back of the truck, shining his flashlight around. We could see that there were other cages in there. The guy found what he was looking for, attached to the wall next to a fire extinguisher: a long, black metal thing. He handed it down to one of the other men.

"That's a jack," said Victor. "They're gonna change the tire."

"How long will that take?" I asked.

"Ten or fifteen minutes, if they know what they're doing. Then they'll be on their way again."

The men were putting the jack under the truck.

"I screwed everything up," said Matt. "By peeing."

"It's okay," I said. "I screwed up, too."

"We all did," said Victor.

"Except me," said Taylor.

"The question is," said Victor, "what do we do now? We still need to stop them."

"Maybe we could get those two road stars that Taylor had," said Matt. "They went into the grass over there." He pointed toward the grass on the side of the street near where the trucks had stopped the first time. It was about halfway between where we were hiding and where the trucks were parked now.

"I don't know," said Victor. "Even if we can get them without being seen, those guys are going to be looking out for us now."

Two of the men had jacked up the truck and were taking off the wheel. The other two were standing by, looking around. A group of four trick-or-treaters walked past. The two lookouts drifted in their direction, giving them the eyeball. The trick-or-treaters steered clear of the truck.

"See?" said Victor. "They're not letting anybody get close."

The men had the wheel off. They started lowering the spare wheel from a space under the truck. Some more trick-or-treaters came by, and again the two lookouts made sure they didn't get close.

"We're running out of time," said Victor. "We need an idea."

Some more trick-or-treaters were coming toward the trucks.

"Okay," I said. "When those kids get near, and the two guys move toward them to scare them off, I'll try to get the road stars."

"Then what?" said Victor.

"I don't know, but at least we'll have the road stars."

Victor nodded.

The trick-or-treaters were getting close. The lookouts started walking their way.

"Go," said Victor.

I sprinted toward the patch of grass where I'd seen the road stars go flying when Taylor got knocked down. Ahead of me I could see the rear truck and two guys changing the tire. They were busy with that and not looking my way. Past them I could see the two lookouts heading toward the trick-or-treaters. So far, so good.

I reached the patch of grass and started looking around frantically. The problem was, it was dark, so I had to lean over and feel the ground with my hands, which was not efficient. I looked up: the trick-or-treaters were veering away from the trucks. The lookouts were turning back toward where I was. One of them beamed his flashlight in my direction. I dropped to my stomach and pressed myself into the grass.

Somehow, I managed not to scream when my right hand came down on the sharp upturned point of a road star.

So at least I found one. That was the good news. Unfortunately, there was also bad news. For one thing, my hand really hurt and was bleeding. For another thing, the two men had the new wheel on the truck and were tightening it. The two lookouts were drifting in my direction, shining their flashlights around. Like maybe one of them had seen me. I pressed myself harder into the grass as the lookouts drifted closer. I realized they were definitely going to see me in another few seconds. I got ready to get up and run.

"Hey! Let's go!"

The lookouts stopped. The tire-changers had finished and were lowering the jack. The lookouts turned around and headed back toward them. Now all four of them were gathered around the back of the second truck.

Which meant nobody was watching the front truck.

Without thinking about it, I stood up. I had a clear path in front of me, and the four guys were not looking my way. All I had to do was get to the front truck, put the road star under the front tire, and keep going. I saw that I definitely was going to make it. I started running.

Then I stepped on the second road star.

This time, I screamed. I couldn't help myself. It went through my sneaker and into my right foot, and it really, seriously hurt. I fell forward onto the street, and the road star I'd been holding flew out of my hands, tumbling toward the front truck. All four hazmat suits were running my way, shouting. I rolled onto my back in the road, moaning. I could feel my right sneaker getting wet with blood. The hazmat men gathered around me, looking really mad. I looked up and saw that one of them—the big one who grabbed me by the arm before—was holding the road star I dropped in the street. He pulled it back, like he was going to throw it at me. I held up my hands to block it. Blood from the cut on my hand dripped down my face.

One of the other guys grabbed the big guy's arm and said, "He's messed up enough already."

"Good," said the big guy.

Out of the corner of my eye, I saw something move behind the men. I turned my head a little to see better. It was Taylor, in her jeans and hoodie, sprinting toward the second truck. *What was she doing?*

"What do we do about him?" said one of the men, I guess meaning about the fact that I was bleeding.

Taylor was at the back of the second truck.

"Leave him," said the first guy. "He got what he deserved. We need to get down there."

The others nodded. The men turned away from me, toward the trucks.

Taylor was gone.

I watched as two of the men went to the first truck and got in. The other two went around behind the second truck, out of my sight. I heard a *bang* sound, which I guessed was them shutting the cargo door. Then they got into the truck cab. Both engines started. The truck behind flashed its lights, they started moving, and a few seconds later were down the street and gone.

I didn't see Taylor. I figured she must have run around behind the trucks and into the yard on the other side.

"Taylor?" I said. "Taylor?" I stood up, which was not easy. My right foot felt like it was on fire.

"TAYLOR?" I yelled.

"Wyatt!"

The voice wasn't Taylor's. It was Matt's. He and Victor were running toward me from the trees.

"Are you okay?" said Matt.

"Where's Taylor?" I said.

"You didn't see?" said Victor.

"No! Where is she?"

"Wyatt," said Victor. "Taylor's on the truck."

CHAPTER 29

What?" I said. "How did she get on the truck?"

"She just jumped on!" said Matt. "Just before those guys started walking toward the back of the truck, she jumped into the back and hid behind one of the crates. The guys didn't even look in there. They just closed the door and took off."

"But why was she even near the truck?"

"I don't know," said Victor. "When you fell down, she said, 'We have to do something!' I said, 'Like what?' And she just said, 'We have to stop them!' and took off running toward the truck. I have no idea what she thought she was going to do."

"She probably didn't have any idea, either," I said.

"Wyatt," said Matt, "you're bleeding a lot."

I looked down at my right hand, which was covered with blood. The streetlight made it look almost black. My right sneaker, which used to be mostly white, was now mostly black. I could feel the blood squishing around down there. I also had blood on my face and all over my shirt.

"You look really messed up," said Matt.

"You need to see a doctor," said Victor.

I shook my head. "Not now. We need to catch up to those guys."

"Wyatt," said Matt. "Victor's right. You need to go to—"

"Just *shut up* about the doctor, okay?" I shouted. "My sister's in trouble, bad trouble, and it's *my fault*. If something happens to her . . ." I had to stop there, because the next thing out of my mouth was going to be a pathetic sob. I bent over and took a few deep breaths, then said, "I'm sorry." I'm not sure who I was saying it to. Matt, I guess, because I yelled at him. But also to Taylor, and my parents, and the world in general. I was just sorry.

"It's okay," said Matt.

I said, "Let's go."

"Go where?" said Victor.

I pointed down the street, where the trucks had gone.

"On foot?" said Victor.

"If we have to," I said. I was feeling pretty desperate, but I figured if I got going instead of standing around, maybe something would happen. So I started walking.

And guess what? Something *did* happen.

I fell down.

My right foot just wouldn't take any weight. I barely got my hands out fast enough to keep my face from smashing into the street.

"Wyatt!" said Matt. "You okay?"

"No," I said. I didn't look up, because I was crying. I was now officially the most pathetic loser on the planet. I couldn't even *try* to help my sister, let alone all the people at the zoo party, which was about to be swarming with Killer Kritters on the wrong side of the cage.

No, instead of doing something, I was going to be lying on my face crying like a baby.

"Wyatt," said Victor. "You need to get up."

"Why?" I said. "What's the point?"

"The point is, you're in the street, and somebody's coming."

I looked up. At the end of the street, a single headlight was heading toward us.

"It's a motorcycle," said Matt.

"The police maybe?" said Victor.

With Victor's help, I stood up and managed to hop to

the side of the street. The light came closer, and we could see it wasn't a police motorcycle. It was a motor scooter, a Vespa. Then it got near the streetlight and we could see who was driving it.

"That's weird," said Victor.

The driver was Chewbacca.

CHAPTER 30

"I s that supposed to be a gorilla?" said Matt.

"No," said Victor. "That's Chewbacca. From *Star Wars*."

"Oh yeah," said Matt. "The Whoopie."

"It's Wookiee," said Victor.

"Really? I always thought it was Whoopie."

"Shut up, Matt," I said as the Wookiee veered our way.

He stopped the scooter right next to us.

"Wyatt?" he said.

"Who're you?" I said.

"Sorry." He turned off the scooter, then took off his Wookiee head, underneath which was Jon. "It's me." He looked at my face and shirt. "Man, you're a mess. What happened?"

"I'll tell you later," I said. "We need to catch the trucks."

"What? They're gone?"

"They just left."

Jon said a bad word. "I was heading for the zoo when I got your text that the trucks were here."

"I'm sorry," I said. "They *were* here. We tried to stop them. It didn't work."

Jon said another bad word.

"It's worse than that," I said. "My sister's in one of the trucks."

"What? With the animals?"

"Yes. I'll explain later. We need to go now. I'll ride on the back." I made a one-foot hop toward the scooter.

He held up his hand. "You can't go."

"Why not?"

"You're hurt, Wyatt. You need to see a doctor."

"I will later."

He shook his head. "You're covered with blood. There's police at the security gate, at the zoo, all over. That's why I had to get this stupid costume, so they won't recognize me. But if I ride past with a bloody kid on the back of the scooter, they're gonna stop me and make me take off the head. Then I'll be arrested." He looked at Matt and Victor. "You're his friends?"

They nodded.

"Get him to a doctor, okay?"

They nodded again.

"I gotta get down to the zoo," he said. He pressed the ignition button and started the scooter. "I should have gone there in the first place."

"Wait!" I said. "You have to take me. That's my sister they have, and it's my fault. *Please*."

"I told you, Wyatt. When the cops see you—"

"What if they can't see me?" I said.

"What do you mean?"

So I told him.

Three minutes later, the Vespa buzzed out through the Bay Estates security gate, past the police officers.

Chewbacca was driving the scooter. Sitting behind him, holding on as best it could, was the front half of a horse.

The officers looked at the scooter, then at each other. Then they shrugged. Another Halloween night in Miami.

CHAPTER

31

"**H**ang on!" shouted Jon, for maybe the fifteenth time.
We were on South Dixie Highway, which is a big six-lane road that always has a lot of traffic. Jon was swerving the scooter left and right, and I was trying to hang on. My right hand still hurt, and my right foot felt like somebody was stabbing it with a screwdriver. I couldn't see very well because I had to look out through the horse's mouth. But I could see that Jon was weaving between cars, ignoring the lane markers. He was also ignoring red lights, blasting right through them. A couple of times we almost got nailed by cars coming from the side. A lot of people were honking at us.

So it was not what I would call a comfortable ride. But we were going faster than the rest of the traffic. Which meant we had to be catching up with the trucks. I hoped.

"Hang on!"

We made a hard right turn. I heard a long honk right next to us.

"Sorry!" shouted Jon, to the honker. To me he shouted, "We're on 152nd Street. We're almost to the zoo." After a few more swerves he yelled, "I see them!"

"The trucks?"

"Yes!" More swerving. "Hang on! We're gonna pass them."

I saw the Gomez Party Rental trucks to our left. I looked at the second one, thinking, *Taylor's in there.* As we went by I leaned the horse head down to the right so Jon's body blocked it, in case the men in the trucks might recognize it. A couple of seconds later we were past the trucks. Jon blasted through another red light, so now we were way in front of them. I sat up and saw the zoo sign ahead on the left. Jon swerved toward it in front of a bunch of honking cars coming the other way.

"What are we doing?" I shouted.

"We're going to where the Killer Kritter party is. We have to tell people to get out of there. We have a little time. The trucks have to go past the zoo and drive around the back."

We turned into the zoo driveway, which was long and

217

had lines of palm trees on both sides. We got to some parking lots that looked pretty full. We zipped past those and onto a walkway leading to the main entrance. There was a ticket booth to the right. Past that was a big archway leading into the zoo, where some employees were standing around. Jon aimed straight for the archway, not slowing down. When the employees saw him coming they started shouting and waving their arms. Jon kept coming, holding the horn button down so it went *beeeeeeeeeeeeep*. The zoo employees jumped out of the way, still shouting as we blasted past them.

We were inside the zoo now, on a wide, straight walkway. Jon kept the horn beeping. People in Halloween costumes scurried out of our way. At the end of the walkway we reached the perimeter path that goes around the whole zoo, past all the exhibits. Jon made a scary sharp right turn onto that, still beeping, still yelling at me to hang on, still swerving like a maniac. I was starting to feel sick. I wanted to take the stupid horse head off but was too afraid to let go. I heard screams and shouts and caught glimpses of people in costumes dodging out of our way. I saw a sign that said INDIAN ELEPHANT, but I didn't see an actual elephant, which was pretty much the only thing that could have made the situation worse.

We kept going. And going. And going. The swerving was making me feel so sick I almost forgot about the road star

218

stabbing my foot. I was pretty sure I was going to barf inside the horse head. Then, suddenly, Jon skidded the scooter to a stop, turned off the engine, and got off. I pulled off the horse head, finally, and saw that we were at the edge of a huge crowd of people in costumes. We had reached the party. Up ahead was a banner that said KILLER KRITTERS hanging over a bunch of cages, with people swarming all around. Next to that was a lit-up stage with a DJ on it, shouting into a microphone.

Jon turned to me and yelled, "I need to get on the PA system!" He started shoving his way through the crowd. I got off the scooter and almost fell down from the pain of my right foot touching the ground. I started hobbling after Jon, using my left foot mainly.

"The walking dead!" A guy dressed as Iron Man was pointing at me. "Nice job!" A bunch of other people looked at me and started laughing. For a second I didn't understand. Then it hit me. I had blood all over my face and arms, and I was walking weird. They thought I was a zombie for Halloween.

I zombied after Jon as best I could, but with my foot on fire I was having trouble keeping up. He got to the edge of the stage and climbed up onto it just as the DJ started playing "Monster Mash."

Jon—who still had his Wookiee head on—ran across the

stage to the DJ, who looked surprised. Jon said something to him, which I couldn't hear, then reached for the microphone. The DJ yanked it back and yelled something. Now the DJ and the Wookiee were struggling for it, and people were starting to notice.

Finally Jon managed to yank the microphone free.

"EVERYONE PLEASE LISTEN!" he shouted, over the sounds of "Monster Mash." "THIS IS AN EMERGENCY! THERE ARE DANGEROUS ANIMALS IN THE AREA! YOU NEED TO LEAVE THE AREA IMMEDIATELY!"

I think Jon seriously thought everybody would listen to him and leave the area. But there were two problems. The first was, everybody already knew there were dangerous animals there, because the exhibit was called Killer Kritters. Dangerous animals were exactly what everybody came to see. Of course, Jon was talking about a *different* bunch of killer kritters, but the crowd didn't know that.

Second, people generally do not expect to get serious information from a guy in a Wookiee costume.

So nobody left the area. A lot of people laughed. I think they thought Jon was part of the entertainment. The DJ was not entertained. He was trying hard to get his microphone back.

"PLEASE," Jon was saying as he shoved the DJ away.

"THIS IS NOT A JOKE. YOU'RE ALL IN DANGER IF YOU STAY HERE!"

I heard shouting behind me. I turned around and saw a police officer coming through the crowd in a hurry. Behind him were two more. They were heading straight for Jon. Somebody must have reported the crazy Wookiee scooter driver.

"YOU HAVE TO LISTEN TO ME!" Jon was shouting.

At that point he seemed to realize that the Wookiee head wasn't helping. He yanked it off and threw it at the DJ, who ducked away. Seeing his face, one of the cops yelled, "That's him!"

"PLEASE LISTEN TO ME!" Jon was shouting into the microphone. "I'M AN AGENT WITH THE U.S. FISH AND WILDLIFE SERVICE, AND I'M TELLING YOU THE TRUTH. DANGEROUS ANIMALS ARE ABOUT TO BE RELEASED IN—"

An officer tackled him before he could finish. Two more jumped on him while he was down. The crowd was shouting, whooping, taking phone videos. There were a few screams. The microphone was rolling across the stage. The DJ grabbed it.

"Everybody calm down!" he said. "Everything is under control! Nothing to worry about, folks."

The police were putting handcuffs on Jon. He was shouting at them, but they weren't listening.

I stood in the crowd, trying to think what I could do. As I stared at Jon's frantic face, something in the background caught my eye. Past the back of the stage, a dozen or so feet away, was the high chain-link fence that went around the zoo property. There was movement on the other side. I shielded my eyes from the stage lights and squinted. Now I could see them—just barely, because their lights were off.

The trucks were arriving.

"Monster Mash" finished playing.

The DJ started a new song.

"Thriller."

CHAPTER 32

I turned around and starting hobbling back through the crowd. Everybody was still looking at the stage, where Jon was still pleading with the police, who were still not listening.

I won't keep bringing this up, but my right foot was still killing me.

I had the beginning of a plan. That was all I had. I had no middle, or ending. So it was probably not going to work.

But it was all I had.

The scooter was where Jon had left it. I looked around. Nobody seemed to be watching. I got on the seat and pressed the ignition button. Nothing happened. I looked down and

223

saw a key. I turned it and tried the button again. The scooter started and the headlight came on.

It took me a few seconds to figure out how to get the scooter down off the parking stand. (If I were still mentioning my foot, I'd mention that this part really hurt.) Then I twisted the throttle thing on the handle, and almost fell off backward when the scooter took off.

I'd never driven a scooter before, but I figured it would be pretty much the same as riding a bicycle. That was not totally true. It's a lot heavier than a bike, and it can get away from you. I almost hit some people and then a bench before I got it under control. Even then I was wobbly, and a couple more times I almost hit people. A few people yelled at me. I yelled "SORRY!" back, but I didn't dare slow down, because there wasn't much time.

I scootered back along the perimeter path to the main walkway, and turned left. I could see the main entrance archway ahead. There were still zoo workers there. This time they saw the scooter from a long way off, and got out of the way when I blasted through yelling "SORRY!" In a few seconds I was going past the parking lot and on the zoo driveway heading out. I reached 152nd Street and turned left—but on the sidewalk, not the street.

The good news was, there were no people on the sidewalk. There were no houses on this side of the street, because it ran along the zoo property. I drove on the sidewalk, looking for the dirt road Jon talked about. I went for what felt like a mile, although it probably was only a hundred yards or so. Then I saw two posts with a chain running between them, and a NO TRESPASSING sign. On the other side was a dirt road. I didn't bother with the chain. I just went around the posts and started down the road.

Pretty soon it went into some woods, so I was in the dark except for the scooter headlight. To my left I could see the chain-link fence that went around the zoo. Up ahead, on the other side of the fence, I saw bright lights, which had to be the stage at the Killer Kritters party.

Which meant I was getting close to the trucks.

Which meant now I had to come up with Part Two of my plan.

I stopped the scooter and fiddled around with the controls until I figured out how to turn off the headlight. Then I started going again, more slowly, steering by the light coming from the stage. The road curved right, then left. And then I saw the trucks, maybe fifty feet ahead of me. I steered the scooter off the road behind some bushes, and stopped the motor. I hobbled forward to take a look.

The trucks were parked next to each other, with the backs facing toward the zoo party. The cargo doors were still shut. The men were still wearing their white hazmat suits, but now they had heavy gloves on, too. I guess to avoid getting bitten. One of the men was talking on a cell phone while the other three watched. The DJ was taking a break, so the stage was quieter. I could hear the guy talking but couldn't make out what he was saying. I figured he was talking to Frank Bevin.

I pulled out my phone to check the time. 9:23. The party would be going on for another hour and a half. Plenty of time for the things in the truck to crawl over there.

Then I noticed that I had a bunch of new texts.

They were all from Taylor.

They all said *call*.

CHAPTER

33

I hobbled back into the bushes and pressed CALL. Taylor answered right away.

"Wyatt, I'm in the truck," she whispered. "With the snakes and stuff."

"I know," I whispered. "I'm here. Near you."

"You are?" She sounded relieved.

"I can see your truck."

"Are we at the zoo?"

"Behind it. Next to where the party is."

"Is help coming?"

"I don't know," I whispered. Which was basically a lie.

227

"Oh." She was quiet for a few seconds. "Can you see what they're doing?"

"Right now one of them is on the phone. I think they're getting ready to unload the trucks. Is there someplace you can hide when they open the door?"

She was quiet again. Then she said, "When they open the door on my truck, stay out of the way."

"Why?"

"I gotta go. Don't want them to hear me."

"Taylor, what are you going to do?"

"Just stay out of the way."

Then she disconnected.

What was she going to do?

I hobbled a little way back out to have another look. The guy on the phone finished his conversation and said some stuff to the other three. Then all four guys went to the first truck, the one Taylor wasn't in. One of them lifted the cargo door. Inside the truck, filling up most of the cargo compartment, was a big shiny metal container, reflecting the lights from the zoo party. That had to be the ants. The side facing out was basically a big door, with latch handles on either side at the top and hinges on the bottom.

The four men climbed into the truck. They squeezed past the container, two on each side. They started shoving it—it looked heavy—and for a second I thought they were going to push it out of the truck. But instead they slid it to the edge of the opening and stopped. Then they went back into the truck and started doing something to lift the back of the container so the front part started leaning forward.

That was when I figured out how they were going to do it.

First, they were going to prop up the back of the container so it was tilted out over the ground. When the door was unlatched, it would fall open and dump out the ant colony, dirt and all.

Then they'd open the back of the second truck. They'd find Taylor inside, of course, but she'd be no problem for four grown men. They'd get her out of the way—*What would they do to Taylor?*—then they'd slide the animal crates to the edge of the truck.

When they were ready, they'd have one guy in the driver's seat of each truck, and one guy in the back of each. The guy in back of the first truck would unlatch the container and dump the ants onto the ground. The guy in the back of the second truck would open the crates and dump out the other animals. Both guys would be safely up in the trucks, not on the ground with the animals. When they were done, the trucks would drive away with the men and the empty cages, leaving all the animals loose behind. The whole thing would take less than a minute.

And maybe a few minutes after that a black mamba

would slither under the fence, into the mass of human legs on the other side. Or maybe it would be a deathstalker scorpion, or a Brazilian wandering spider. Or even the Komodo dragon.

Maybe the ants would head that way. I remembered what Jon said.

When the driver ants come out, after being cooped up in there . . . You would not want to be in their way.

People would panic, and the panic would spread fast. People would be injured. Or worse. Way worse.

It was only a matter of time, unless somebody stopped the men with the trucks.

But there was nobody around to stop them except me, a kid who could barely walk. And there was no way now I could stop them from letting the animals go. That battle was lost. The only thing I could do was try to get Taylor out of there. I decided I'd wait until they were opening the door, then charge them on the scooter. Maybe I could take them by surprise, throw them off-balance, and Taylor could jump on the back and we could get out of there.

It wasn't brilliant. But it was the only plan I could think of. I hobbled over and got back on the scooter. The four men were still working on the ant container, trying to get it propped up. They were struggling with the weight, but they were getting there.

The DJ had started playing music again. He put on "Werewolves of London." It's an old song, and I don't totally understand it, but I always liked it. It's kind of crazy.

"*AOOOOO!*" went the singer. "*AOOOOO!*"

I was hearing that, watching the men in the truck, waiting to make my rescue attempt, when I felt a tap on my shoulder. I jumped and turned around so fast I almost dropped the scooter.

"Hey," said Suzana Delgado.

CHAPTER 34

"**Y**ou're here," I said, when I could finally talk.

"Apparently," she said. "What happened to you? You look horrible."

"I'll explain later. Why are you here?"

"I did what you said. I didn't want to, but you pissed me off so much, telling me I was wrong about the Bevin brothers, that I decided to prove *you* were wrong. So I told them I wanted to go to the zoo party."

"And?"

"They totally freaked out. They basically *ordered* me not to come here. But I insisted, so they said, 'Okay, we'll give you a ride to the zoo.' They picked me up at my house, but instead of taking me here, they took me to the Grove and followed me around, making sure I didn't leave. Can you believe that? They *kidnapped* me. Jerks."

"So what'd you do?"

"I escaped. Said I needed the ladies' room, went into a restaurant, and snuck out the back. Got a ride with some Coral Cove kids headed this way. They dropped me off at the end of the dirt road. I ran the rest of the way."

Suzana, in addition to being the prettiest girl at Coral Cove and probably on earth, is a really good soccer player who can basically outrun a Ferrari.

"So what's happening?" she said, pointing ahead at the men. "Are the poison things in those trucks?"

"Them, and my sister."

"*What?*"

I explained, as fast as I could, what was going on, what I thought was going to happen, and how I planned to try to rescue Taylor. Fortunately, Suzana, in addition to being beautiful and athletic, is really smart, so she followed me, no problem.

"Okay," she said. "Your plan is stupid."

I should mention that, in addition to being beautiful, athletic, and smart, she has strong opinions.

"Why?" I said.

"They'll knock you off the scooter. They'll grab you and

your sister, and they'll probably feed you to the ants. They're not going to let witnesses get away."

"Oh."

"Also," she said, "it's not just about rescuing your sister. We can't let them release the animals."

"So what do we—"

"Let me think," said Suzana, holding up her hand. Ahead, the men had finished propping up the ant container, which was now leaning out over the ground. One of them unlatched the latch on the upper left side, so that when they were ready to go, they'd only have to unlatch the right side. The men were climbing down from the back of the truck. Now they'd go over to the second truck, and they'd find Taylor.

"Okay," said Suzana, apparently done thinking. "Get out your phone."

"What? Why?"

"Just get it out, and do what I do."

I got out my phone. I had no idea why.

The men were at the second truck now. One of them started to lift the cargo door.

"HOLD IT!" shouted Suzana. She left the bushes and started walking their way. She was holding her phone in front of her, aiming the camera toward the men. I hobbled out behind her, holding up my phone. The men were staring at us. The one guy still had his hand on the cargo door.

"WE'RE LIVE-STREAMING YOU," shouted Suzana. "DO YOU UNDERSTAND WHAT THAT MEANS? EVERYTHING YOU'RE DOING NOW IS BEING TRANSMITTED OVER THE INTERNET AND RECORDED IN A REMOTE LOCATION. IF YOU LET THOSE ANIMALS GO, THERE WILL BE A VIDEO RECORD OF YOUR CRIME."

Of course I wasn't live-streaming anything. I didn't think Suzana was, either. She didn't have time to set it up.

Three of the men looked toward the one who'd been on the phone before. Apparently he was the leader. And apparently he had decided Suzana was bluffing.

"You two," he said to the two men closest to us. "Grab them."

They started toward us.

"YOU'RE MAKING A MISTAKE!" shouted Suzana.

The men kept coming.

Behind them, the man at the back of the truck finished opening the cargo door.

Then he shouted, "HEY!"

Then a thick white cloud of fog came *whoosh*ing out of the back of the truck, surrounding the men. The door guy shouted "HEY" again, and then there was a loud *CLONK*. Suddenly the door guy was lying on the ground. There was more shouting and another *CLONK*. Now the leader was also on the ground.

The two guys who had been heading toward me and Suzana spun around and ran back toward the truck. They plunged into the fog, and I heard Taylor yell, "Let me go!" One of the guys came staggering out, with his arms around Taylor, who was still yelling. She was holding a fire extinguisher that was still shooting out fog. The other guy yanked it away from her, shut it off, and threw it into the woods.

Everybody stood still for a few seconds. The fire-extinguisher fog melted away, and by the lights from the zoo stage, we could see the situation. Two of Bevin's guys were now on the ground, having been clonked on the head with a fire extinguisher by my little sister. One guy was moaning and holding his head, which was bleeding. The other—the leader—was out cold.

But the two remaining guys were okay. And one was holding Taylor. He had his arm across her neck. He was looking at me and Suzana.

"Hand over the phones," he said.

"Don't do it!" said Taylor.

"Shut up!" said the guy. He squeezed Taylor's neck. Suzana and I looked at each other.

"Okay," I said. We handed our phones to the other guy, who threw them on the ground and stomped on them.

I just want to say that, even when there are really bad things going on—things that are much worse than losing some electronic gadget—it still hurts to see your phone get smashed.

"All right," said the guy holding Taylor, like he was about to say something important. But he didn't. He just looked at the other guy, who looked back. I realized they didn't know what to do.

And then I heard myself speaking up.

"Just go," I said. "Just leave. You can't do your plan. You need four guys. You can't do it now. So just take your friends and go. You can get away. Go."

It was definitely the best speech I ever gave. I could see the two guys thinking about it and realizing I was right. With two of them, including their leader, down, their best bet was to just get out of there. They looked at each other and nodded. The guy holding Taylor let her go. She ran over to where Suzana and I were standing.

The two guys went over to the leader. They grabbed him under his arms, picked him up, and dragged him over to the first truck. They lifted him into the cab and closed the door. Then they helped the other guy, who was conscious but really woozy, into the second truck.

The two guys, hurrying now, went to the driver's sides of the trucks and got in. It hit me then: they were going to leave. We had stopped them. Actually, to be honest, Taylor had stopped them, and I knew she was never, ever going to let me forget it. But I didn't care. The point was, we had won.

The men started the engines.

It was over.

Then I heard a third engine, behind me.

I turned around. A car, headlights out, was coming, fast. As it got closer I saw it was a black Jeep Wrangler, all tricked out, with huge tires and a Miami Heat logo on the hood.

It skidded to a stop right in front of us. The doors opened fast.

Out jumped Frank, Nick, and Troy Bevin.

CHAPTER

35

Frank Bevin was by the trucks, talking to the two guys who didn't get knocked out by Taylor. He was very unhappy with them.

I was by the bushes with Suzana and Taylor. Nick and Troy stood a few yards away.

"You guys run," I whispered. "Maybe you can get help."

"I'm staying," said Suzana.

"Me too," said Taylor.

The truth was, even if they did run, they probably wouldn't have gotten away from the Bevin brothers, who were staring at us. Troy was staring especially hard at Suzana.

"You should have listened to us," he said. "You made a big mistake. A really big mistake."

She shook her head. "My mistake was not realizing how disgusting you two are."

Troy was about to say something else when his father came over. He didn't even look at us.

"Okay," he said. "These idiots screwed it up, so we're going to have to do this ourselves. Troy, you'll be in the right-hand truck. When I tell you, you'll open those cages as fast as you can and dump the animals out. Be careful, and wear these." He handed Troy a pair of gloves that he'd gotten from one of the other men.

"Nick, you'll be in the other truck. Get on the right side. You see the latch handle?"

Nick looked at the truck with the ant container and nodded.

"When Troy's almost done, I'll give you the signal, and you pull that handle. That'll dump the ants. You stay up in the truck, out of the way, got it?"

Nick nodded again.

"As soon as they're all dumped out I'll honk the Jeep horn, and the men will drive the trucks out of here. You two stay in the back. I'll follow in the Jeep. When we get to 152nd Street, we'll all stop and you two can get back in the Jeep. Got it?"

Troy and Nick nodded. Then Nick pointed to us and said, "What about them?"

Frank Bevin answered without looking at us. "What *about* them?"

"Well," said Nick, "I mean they know about . . ." He waved his arms toward the trucks. "All this."

"Yes," said Frank. "But in five minutes, all *this* will be gone. So you'll have three kids—including a known thief— telling some crazy story about one of the most respected men in the community. I'm not worried about them." Now, for the first time, he looked at us, the way a man looks at a bug. "Although," he said, "if I were them, I'd start running."

"He can't run!" said Taylor, pointing at me. "He's hurt! He can't even walk!"

"How unfortunate for him," said Frank, turning away. "Okay, boys. Let's do this." He walked over and said something to the two drivers. Troy headed toward the near truck, with the cages. Nick headed for the truck with the ant container. They weren't worried about us anymore.

"We need to get out of here before they let those things loose," I said.

"You can't walk!" said Taylor.

"The scooter," I said.

"What scooter?" said Taylor.

"It's Jon's," I said. "I rode it here. It's in those bushes.

Maybe we can all squeeze on it." I started to hobble toward it, but Suzana didn't move.

"Suzana," I said, "we can't stay here."

She was staring at the trucks. Nick and Troy were climbing up into the truck backs. The two drivers were climbing into the cabs. Frank was heading toward the Jeep.

"We can't just let them win!" she said. She looked around, then picked up a rock.

"Suzana!" I said. "That's not going to stop them!"

"What about this?" said Taylor. She was pulling something from the pocket of her hoodie. It looked like a stick of dynamite, a red thing about a foot long with a bunch of words printed on it.

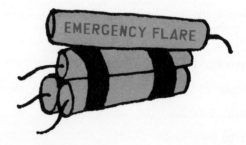

"What's that?" said Suzana.

"An emergency flare," she said. "I found it in the truck. I was going to use it to fight them, before I found the fire extinguisher."

Suzana dropped the rock. "How do you work it?" she said.

CHAPTER 36

F rank was standing next to the Jeep. "Troy!" he shouted. "You ready?"

Troy gave the thumbs-up. He was up in the back of the right-hand truck, standing next to the cage with the Komodo dragon inside. On his other side were a bunch of smaller cages, ready to be unloaded.

"Nick!" shouted Frank. "Ready?"

Nick nodded. He was standing in the back of the other truck, next to the ant container. He had his hand on the right-hand latch handle, ready to pull.

We were only a few dozen feet from the zoo fence, but

Frank could yell as loud as he wanted. Nobody at the Killer Kritter party could hear him over the sound of the crowd noise and the DJ, who was now blasting another old Halloween-y song, "(Don't Fear) The Reaper."

"All right, Troy," shouted Frank. "Let them go!"

Troy leaned over and started to undo the latch on the Komodo dragon cage.

That's when the scooter came bursting out of the bushes, headlight on, horn beeping.

I was driving. Taylor was sitting behind me. Sitting behind her was Suzana, holding up the flare like it was the Olympic torch. It was burning with a bright reddish-orange light, and there was a lot of smoke billowing out.

I swerved close to Frank, who grabbed for the scooter but missed. He started yelling and running after us as I swerved toward the truck with Troy in it. Suzana faked like she was going to throw the flare at him. He flinched and jumped back. I kept going. Now Troy was out of the truck and chasing us, too. I swerved toward the truck with Nick in it. I stopped the scooter right in front of him. He was standing with his hand on the latch handle, looking confused. I glanced back. Frank and Troy were almost on us.

"GO!" yelled Suzana, and at the same time, threw the flare at Nick.

Nick, who is very athletic, saw it coming and reacted in

244

time. He jumped to his right, hanging on to keep from falling out of the truck. The flare sailed past him, past the ant container, and into the truck cargo area. So Nick would have been fine, except for one problem.

The thing he was hanging on to was the latch handle.

Nick's weight pulled it down, unlatching the container door. With Nick still holding on, it fell open. Out poured the contents: a big pile of dirt and several million really unhappy siafu ants.

They flew through the air and landed, like raindrops with really strong little jaws, not just on Nick, but also on Troy and Frank, who arrived just as the scooter pulled away. More ants swarmed up from the dirt pile. That's when the screaming started.

I drove a little way and turned the scooter around so we could see what was happening. This wasn't what we had expected to happen. If we had tried fourteen million times on purpose to make this happen, we would have failed fourteen million times. We were just hoping to hassle the Bevins, and draw somebody's attention with the flare. We hadn't planned for the ants to get loose. They were swarming on the Bevins, who were screaming and brushing wildly at their legs and arms as they ran away from the dirt pile.

Meanwhile the ant truck was now on fire. Smoke and flames were shooting out of the cargo area. The driver jumped out his side, ran around to the other side, and pulled out one of the guys Taylor had clonked. They staggered over to the Jeep, where they were joined by the two guys from the other truck. The four of them got in the Jeep and roared away. They didn't seem too concerned about the Bevins.

Flames from the truck were shooting toward the sky. In the distance I heard sirens.

The Bevins were still screaming and flailing. They were on their feet and moving. They were going to survive. But they were definitely in a tremendous amount of pain.

I admit I smiled as I twisted the scooter throttle.

CHAPTER

37

Here's what happened after we left:

First the fire department arrived. They put out the truck fire, but they also noticed the ant pile and the Bevins, who by then were begging for medical attention. The firefighters called in paramedics to take care of the Bevins, and some guys who sprayed stuff on the ant pile, which took care of most of the ants.

Of course the firefighters also noticed the other truck and the cages full of weird animals. They figured it must have something to do with the zoo, so they they called some zoo people, who got there quickly, since they were right next door.

The zoo people were *very* interested in the animals on the truck. They called the police and other agencies, so pretty soon there was a major investigation going on. It led quickly to the four guys in the Jeep, and to Frank Bevin, and from there to some other very important people who suddenly needed very expensive lawyers.

I'll skip over a bunch of boring legal stuff that happened after that. Basically, Frank Bevin is in big trouble and is almost definitely going to prison. Nick and Troy probably won't go to prison, but they're no longer at Coral Cove High. They're attending some kind of disciplinary school in someplace cold—I think maybe Maine. It doesn't have a football team.

Frank Bevin's MegaDade project is definitely not going to happen. The zoo expansion is.

Speaking of the zoo, it's now the new home of the animals that were on the truck. The Komodo dragon, which is a lot bigger than the one the zoo already had, has become one of the most popular exhibits. They named it Zevon.

Jon Aibel is back with the U.S. Fish and Wildlife Service. He even got promoted. He's still friends with Taylor and me and sometimes visits us, only now he comes in by the front door. Taylor is still in love with him, although she accepted the fact that she'll probably have to wait another ten or fifteen years before the timing is right. Jon did promise her that, if they ever come to town and it's okay with my parents, he'll take her to see Snot House.

Speaking of Taylor, she's still incredibly annoying. Maybe even more annoying than before, because now, on top of everything else, she can point out that she was the hero who saved the day, and she points this out a lot. But the truth is, she *did* save the day. And she believed me when hardly anybody else did. So even though she's annoying, I have to say that I'm glad she's my sister. Most of the time.

As for me, I had a lot to explain when I got home Halloween night looking like a blood-covered zombie, and my parents discovered that the sulky, pouty teenager they'd been communicating with through my bedroom door was not me but Dylan Schweitzer. My mom yelled at me all the way to the emergency room, where I had to get a tetanus shot and stitches in my foot and crutches, although basically I was okay. While we were at the hospital the police showed up, which was good, because the police backed up what Taylor and I were saying. It took a while for all the details to come out, and my parents were really upset about certain things, like the part about Taylor in the truck. But once they had the whole story, they were pretty proud of us, and I think they felt guilty about believing I was a thief. So now that it's all over, things are pretty good between me and my parents, if you don't count the fact that I'm still doing bad in Trigonometry.

Things are also pretty good between Suzana and me. We're not boyfriend and girlfriend or anything, but we're definitely friends again, maybe better friends than we were. And I think someday we *could* maybe be boyfriend and girlfriend, which is an interesting thing to think about. I'm getting to know more kids at Coral Cove, which feels a lot friendlier these days, now that the Bevins are gone.

The other day before school I was in the courtyard with Matt and Victor, and The Stinger walked by us and stopped. Usually this is a bad thing. I automatically looked down to see what dress code violation I was guilty of. But instead of giving me a detention, she said, "Mr. Palmer, are you staying out of trouble?"

"Yes," I said. "Totally."

"Good," she said. "Only three and a half years to go."

I won't say she smiled then, because I don't believe that The Stinger is physically capable of smiling. But for just a fraction of a second there, she looked a tiny bit less unhappy than usual.

I think it's going to be a pretty good year.